THE TIDES HAVE TURNED.

Your precious Alpha team has failed you. They were unable to retrieve the third element for the Source that will save your planet. But my team— the Omega team—has succeeded in every challenge so far and will return to Earth the true winners. Yes, Team Omega will return with the Source, and you can save your planet . . . for a price.

Alpha should be prepared to pay, or your planet will go dark.

Colin, Consulting Commander
Omega Team

Beneath the surface of Infinity, there are laboratories.

And scientists who will study
any and all creatures they encounter.

Including a few members of the
human species who are about to arrive.

INFINITY RIDERS

VOYAGERS

Don't miss a single Voyage. . . .

VOYAGERS

INFINITY RIDERS

Kekla Magoon

Random House 🏠 New York

Copyright © 2016 by PC Studios Inc.
Full-color interior art, puzzles, and codes copyright © Animal Repair Shop
Voyagers digital and gaming experience by Animal Repair Shop

All rights reserved. Published in the United States by Random House
Children's Books, a division of Penguin Random House LLC, New York.

Random House and the colophon are registered trademarks of
Penguin Random House LLC.

Visit us on the Web! randomhousekids.com

Educators and librarians, for a variety of teaching tools, visit us at
RHTeachersLibrarians.com

VoyagersHQ.com

Library of Congress Cataloging-in-Publication Data
is available upon request.

ISBN 978-0-385-38667-8 (trade)—ISBN 978-0-385-38669-2 (lib. bdg.)
ISBN 978-0-385-38668-5 (ebook)

Printed in the United States of America
10 9 8 7 6 5 4 3 2 1
First Edition

Random House Children's Books supports the First Amendment

and celebrates the right to read.

FOR T.T.

"**Prepare to exit** Gamma Speed," chirped a bright voice on the flight deck of the *Cloud Leopard.*

STEAM 6000, a three-foot-tall, oval-headed robot, punched a series of buttons on the spaceship's console. "All life-forms, prepare for rapid deceleration lest you be hurtled into oblivion."

Dash Conroy glanced up from the comic book he was reading and smiled. "Thanks, STEAM," he said. "I'll let everyone know."

"That's what you said ten minutes ago," STEAM chided. "Now it is really the time, yes sir."

Dash flipped ahead in the comic, scanning for a good stopping point. "How long until we get there?"

"Entering orbit around planet Infinity in . . . countdown: ten minutes . . . ," the robot verified. "Nine minutes fifty-nine seconds . . . nine fifty-eight . . . nine fifty-seven . . ."

"Whoa," said Dash. He laid the comic over the

arm of his chair to hold his place. Only nine minutes to get everyone rounded up and secure?

He slid out of the captain's chair, his heart already thumping with anticipation. The *Cloud Leopard* crew was about to arrive at the fourth stop on their six-planet tour of the universe. Each new planet so far had brought a unique blend of mystery and danger. It was time to get ready . . . for anything.

Dash hurried toward a panel on the wall. He studied the map of the tunnel system the crew used for traveling around the ship.

"No time for games." STEAM waddled over to Dash. "Prepare to exit Gamma Speed, in nine minutes twenty-six seconds, yes sir," the robot said. "Nine twenty-five . . . get a move on, sir; you better shake your bacon."

The robot's quirky chiding nudged Dash out of his strategizing. "Sure. Thanks, pal."

"That is what friends are for, yes sir." STEAM went back to work. A crew of ZRKs buzzed alongside him, busily helping out. The golf ball–sized robot assistants darted and hovered, extending their mechanical arms here and there to tinker with things.

Dash traced his finger over the map in the longest path he could think of. Oops, force of habit. He shrugged. Sure, he had to hurry, but taking a few extra seconds to try for the record wouldn't hurt anything. The panel opened, and he plunged himself feetfirst into the tunnel. Moments later, after a whooshing, winding ride, Dash shot out of the tunnel and landed in the crew's recreation room. He smoothed down the sleeves of his flight suit and checked his distance—good, but not good enough to overtake the record.

Dang.

A smiling black-haired girl sat cross-legged in the middle of the carpet, speaking Japanese to a two-foot-tall, squarish robot.

"Hey, Carly! Hi, TULIP," Dash said. "We're almost to the next planet."

"Hiya, Dash," Carly Diamond said.

TULIP beeped and squawked in greeting. The small robot's belly glowed, a side effect of the gallon of molten metal she carried. She radiated warmth.

Carly glanced past Dash, toward the tube system. "Ha," she said. "I'm still in the lead." Ever since they first boarded the *Cloud Leopard* nearly nine months ago, the crew had been competing to find the longest tunnel path between two points on the spaceship.

TULIP beeped, as if to cheer. Carly and TULIP had been spending a lot of time together lately. The small robot didn't speak any human language, but talking to TULIP in her own first language made Carly feel at home.

"Yeah, yeah." Dash grinned at the pair of them. "We're about to arrive at Infinity," he told Carly. "Report to the flight deck, pronto."

TULIP whistled softly, perhaps in response to Dash's unusually urgent tone. Carly smiled at the slogger. Then to Dash she said, "I'll head right up."

A soft, vibrating alarm began sounding from the Mobile Tech Band attached to Dash's arm like a sleeve. He quickly silenced it.

"What was that?" Carly asked.

"It's nothing," Dash lied. He wished she hadn't noticed the alarm. He had it set to vibrate for a reason. Only Chris and Piper knew about his need for daily shots, and he wanted to keep it that way. The reminder alarm usually took precedence over anything, but right now, STEAM's countdown echoed in Dash's head. The ship's course was predetermined. It would stop whether the crew was strapped in or not. Being hurtled into oblivion would not be a great outcome.

"Let's get ready to stop," he said.

"Right," Carly agreed, getting to her feet.

"I'll get Chris," Dash told her. "Have you seen Piper or Gabriel?"

"Piper was in our room a little while ago. I'll see if she's still there," Carly said, and zoomed off through the tunnels.

Dash reset the alarm on his MTB for the following

day. He felt guilty about keeping this secret from his friends. Every day, he considered telling them the truth: the shots were saving his life. But he also didn't want to worry them unnecessarily.

He rode the tunnels to the ship's lower level, emerging in the corridor outside the engine room. It still wasn't the longest path through the tunnels, but Dash was sure he was getting closer.

Dash hurried toward Chris's quarters. As he passed the training room, Dash heard the sounds of an argument coming from inside. He punched the door release and rushed into the room.

"Traitor!" Piper Williams said.

"You're the traitor," Gabriel's voice responded angrily. "My revenge will be sweet."

Gabriel Parker stood at one end of the room. On the other side, Piper hovered in her air chair, the space-friendly gadget that took the place of the wheelchair she used back on Earth. Both were armed with very long swords. They were so focused on each other that they didn't notice Dash enter.

"Guys—" Dash started, but his voice was drowned out.

"Prepare to die!" Piper yelled. She zoomed toward Gabriel at top speed, her blond hair whipping behind her. Gabriel ran forward to meet her. Dash dove backward, pressing himself against the wall to get out of the way. His heart raced strangely fast.

Was it nerves? Adrenaline? He breathed deeply to steady himself.

The swords clashed in a sickening crunch. Then both fighters pulled back for a second shot. They swung swords toward each other again, but at the last second, Piper twisted her chair sharply to the side. Gabriel's blade strike caught the metal arm of her chair. With a victorious whoop, Piper reached down and drove the tip of her sword into his stomach.

2

Gabriel buckled and groaned loudly, crashing to the floor. Well, bouncing to the floor was more like it. The room was padded with gymnastic mats, and both he and Piper were dressed in comically-thick foam sparring suits. They looked like miniature sumo wrestlers. Piper had just barely been able to stuff herself into her air chair, which now looked like an overfull laundry basket floating in midair. An overfull laundry basket with a face.

Dash started laughing. "Nice shot, Piper," he said. "Nice, err . . . tumble, Gabe."

Gabriel flopped over onto his back and flailed his arms and legs, unable to roll over and get up. "Falling well is a skill, and don't you forget it," he said, raising a finger. It seemed to be the only part of his body he could effectively move.

"I think you have it mastered," Dash said.

Gabriel shot him a good-natured dirty look.

Then he glared at Piper. "No fair—that chair is like armor," he protested. "I call foul."

"It'll be with me in real combat," Piper argued cheerfully. "That makes it fair game." She sheathed her blunt-tipped sword alongside the air chair and swooped down beside Gabriel. She offered him her hand and helped him stand up.

Dash grinned. "I'm with Piper. All's fair in war . . . and the Simulation Suit."

Gabriel staggered to his feet. "The best part about using these Simu Suits is taking them off after." He started to unzip, revealing his Voyagers uniform underneath. He tucked in the arms and legs of the Simu Suit and then kept folding it in half. As he pressed on each fold, the two-inch-thick foam suit grew thinner and thinner. It folded up remarkably small for something so thick. Gabriel carefully stuffed the suit into a flat black pouch that was barely bigger than a pencil case.

"What are you guys doing, anyway?" Dash asked. He picked up Gabriel's discarded sword. "What's with these new swords? How come you're not using the regular fencing gear?"

The Simu Suits had typically been used for wrestling and other mobility training. If you could learn to move and fight wearing one of those suckers, you could move way faster when you only had your own body to worry about.

"Chris gave them to us," Piper said. "He said we might need them soon."

Dash felt a surge of frustration. "That's weird," he told them. "He never said anything about this to me." Dash studied the sword. It was long, like a fencing foil, but not as thin or flexible. It was flat and wide at the hilt and tapered to a wicked point. Luckily, it had been blunted with a ball of metal for sparring purposes.

"Were you looking for us?" Piper said.

Dash nodded. "We're nearly to Infinity."

"Meet you on the flight deck?" Gabriel asked.

"Yup. And go direct," Dash ordered as he spun toward the door. "No time for winding through the tunnels." The contest was good-natured fun between the crew members, but Dash still wanted to win. And Chris, the crew's alien chaperone, had hinted that there would be some kind of reward or prize for the person who discovered the longest path.

"Yeah right," Gabriel called after him. "Like I'm going to fall for that one."

Dash grinned. He rushed into the hall, heading toward Chris's quarters.

He knocked on the door.

It was opened almost immediately by a blond teenage boy. At least, that's how it appeared. Chris was actually much older than he looked, and he came from a distant planet known as Flora.

"Here for your injection?" Chris said.

"After the Gamma jump," Dash said. "It's time."

Chris frowned and went to the cabinet where he kept his stash of the age serum. "The injection timing is very important," he reminded Dash.

"So is not being pounded to smithereens by the brakes on this thing," Dash commented. But Chris seemed to be taking his time anyway. "We only have a couple of minutes," Dash informed him. Fewer than five, by his inner counting. Which could be off base. It could be even less.

A happy golden retriever bounded off Chris's bed and came to stand by Dash as he waited.

"Hey there, Rocket." Dash ruffled the dog's fur. Rocket was Chris's dog, but he had become something of a team mascot for the whole crew. "You'll have to go in your crate for the Gamma jump, okay?"

Rocket snuffled a protest against Dash's leg.

"Trust me, I feel your pain," Dash assured him.

"It's for your own protection," Chris commented. He could have been talking to Rocket, or he could have been talking about the syringe he was about to inject into Dash.

The rest of the crew had no idea about the risk Dash had taken in agreeing to join the mission. Gabriel, Carly, and Piper had all been twelve years old when they left Earth. As long as the mission lasted a year or less, they'd return safely. But Dash was several months older—too old for safe travel at Gamma Speed. So Dash had to take injections filled with an age-slowing serum to fool his cells into thinking he wasn't aging at all.

Commander Shawn Phillips, the man back on Earth who had orchestrated the Voyagers mission, had taken a serious gamble by putting Dash in charge. But he had believed strongly in Dash's leadership capability. The Voyagers mission had the best shot at success with Dash at the helm. It was worth the risk, they had agreed.

After the last planet, Dash had broken down and told Piper about the serum. It had caused a bit of tension actually. As the ship's medic, Piper wanted to control Dash's injections, but Chris felt it was his responsibility. Dash had left the serum with Chris. He didn't want Piper to have to sneak around. He hoped his choice hadn't hurt her feelings too badly.

Dash rolled up his sleeve. Chris held up the clean syringe. Dash reached for it, prepared to inject himself as usual, but Chris pulled it away. "You're pretty bruised," he said, studying Dash's bare left bicep. The skin was mottled faintly purple and yellow. Chris kept the syringe. "Give that side a break. I'll do it in the other arm."

Dash wiped a spot on his right arm with an

alcohol swab, then turned his head away while Chris administered the injection. He felt like a little kid for doing it, but not looking really did make the shot a little less painful. His other arm did ache from the repetitive injections, but he would've died before admitting it.

"There. That'll keep you young for the next day or so," Chris said. Dash rubbed the spot with the swab again, lifting away the bead of blood that had formed on the skin.

"We have to get up to the flight deck," Dash repeated. "We'll arrive at Infinity any minute."

"Well, that's good," said Chris in a tone that suggested otherwise.

Dash's smile slipped a notch. "What's wrong?" he asked.

"It's all taking somewhat longer than expected," Chris said. "You hadn't noticed?"

Dash shrugged. "I've been kinda busy fighting Raptogons, solving Meta Prime, and negotiating with the AquaGens."

"Yes, I suppose," Chris murmured. "It's my job—and the ship's job—to keep us on time."

"We're doing great," Dash said. But he wasn't as confident as he sounded. They had a Raptogon tooth from J-16 and a slogger full of Magnus 7 from Meta Prime, but they hadn't gotten the Pollen Slither they needed from Aqua Gen. Still, it wasn't *entirely* out of reach. . . .

"We're doing really great," Dash repeated, as if trying to convince himself. "Aren't we?"

Rocket nosed himself closer to Dash. Like most dogs, he had a sixth sense for when someone was about to need some comfort.

Chris looked grim. "Look at your serum stock," he said, waving his hand over the box where he kept the loaded syringes. "How much remains?"

"I dunno. . . . I guess I've used more than I have left," Dash said slowly, realizing it as he spoke. Chris was in charge of Dash's entire supply. Early in the trip, he'd moved the stash from the boys' dorm so that Gabriel wouldn't stumble upon it.

"And yet, the mission is barely half over," Chris said. His voice was heavy. "Only three planets done, and three still to go."

"It'll be fine," Dash said. "You can make more of it, can't you?" Chris was the one who had designed the biologic injection in the first place.

"I don't think you understand," Chris said. "You can't take the age serum indefinitely. If this mission isn't completed in the next eighty-four days, you'll be dead."

3

Dash felt a whole new level of urgency as he and Chris raced to join the rest of the crew gathered on the flight deck. Eighty-four days until his supply of injections ran out. That was less than three months. They had already been traveling for nine.

Would he ever make it back to Earth? The mission was supposed to last one year only. Commander Phillips had been clear about that from the beginning.

Dash knew all along that he was taking a risk with the age serum, sure, but the timing was one thing Dash had never fully stopped to consider. He knew they'd fallen a bit behind schedule. Now he understood the delay could have life-or-death consequences.

The *Cloud Leopard* main computer began a slow, high-pitched whine. Over the warning alarm, STEAM recited, "Exiting Gamma Speed in sixty seconds."

"All right, let's buckle up," Dash said. The crew members climbed into their flight seats and strapped in for the quick deceleration.

"I hate this part," Carly grumbled. The sudden jolt out of Gamma Speed was always a bit harsh.

"I love it," Gabriel said. To him, the Gamma jump was like a really awesome roller coaster ride, where his stomach felt like it flew up into his mouth for a second. It was all slightly painful, but what a rush!

"Here we go," said Piper, gripping the arms of her seat.

The entire *Cloud Leopard* shook and rumbled. The crew pitched forward against their secured seat belts as the speeding ship slammed on its brakes.

"Yeah!" Gabriel whooped once his stomach slowed its churning. "What a ride!" He was the crew's pilot for a reason.

Dash watched on the large monitor screen above the control panel as the *Cloud Leopard* settled into orbit around Infinity.

The thin atmosphere supported no clouds. The air was completely clear. Dash had near perfect visibility of the harsh, rocky, grayish landscape below. He saw no water, no plants. Nothing that seemed to be moving at all.

"You mentioned life on this planet, right?" Dash asked. He turned away from the monitor and clicked out of his flight seat. The crew gathered around the table for the planet briefing. They had been training for certain aspects of the mission during the months-long Gamma jump, but now they would learn the specific details about the tasks they must complete on Infinity.

"There is life," Chris said. "Underground."

"Underground?" Piper said nervously.

"Yes," Chris continued. "The planet is entirely comprised of dense rock. So dense that the gravitational force is increased. Nothing much would survive on the surface. But down below, there is a vast network of tunnels and caves."

"How many things live in the caves?" Gabriel asked.

"Three creatures that I know of. And the element we need to retrieve comes from one of these life-forms."

On the monitor, a batlike creature appeared. The only difference was, each "bat" had a two-foot-long snaking tail that ended in a sharp arrow point.

"These are Stingers," Chris said. "They live in the lake caverns on Infinity."

"Cool," Gabriel said. He thought the creature looked like a cross between a bat and a stingray.

"See those barbs on their tails?" Chris explained. "When Stingers sting, they inject a spore—a small, toxic pellet—into their prey." The screen displayed a single black sphere about the size of a BB. "The spore disintegrates into about a hundred micro-beads of the primary toxin, which then spread through the victim's bloodstream."

"How toxic?" Carly asked.

"Probably lethal to humans," Chris said. "But Stinger spores are the element we need to gather. At least a thousand of them."

"A thousand?" Piper said. That sounded like a lot of lethal stinging action. As the team's medic, she realized they had better find out for sure if the toxin would kill them.

"Yes," Chris said. "We need a hundred thou-sand units of the primary toxin, and there are one hundred per spore."

"How do we catch them?" Dash asked.

"Nets," Chris said. "You'll need to gather enough Stingers and then carefully extract the spores."

"So, scoop some Stingers and don't get stung," Gabriel said. "We got this."

Chris nodded. "You could put it like that."

"Why do I feel like it's not going to be that sim-ple?" Carly asked.

"Two other life-forms to worry about, remem-ber?" Piper said. "What are they?"

"Sawtooth Land Eels, for one," Chris said. The new image that appeared on the monitor caused the crew to gasp.

"Whoa," Gabriel said. "That is one ugly snake."

The creature had a slimy gray-green body. It wasn't scaly, but smooth and greasy-looking, from its thick head all the way to its tapered tail. Its jaws jutted forward, sporting a row of protruding top teeth, all jagged and slightly curved like fangs. In the screen simulation, the creature slithered forward, chomped, and then its jaws ground together in a side-to-side sawing motion. It didn't appear to have eyes. Just teeth.

"The screen doesn't do it justice," Chris commented. "They are large. Ten to twenty feet in diameter and up to a hundred feet in length."

"Ten feet? That's as tall as a school bus," Dash said. "Yikes."

"One to two school buses stacked, yes sir," STEAM reported, whirring quickly though the calculations. "And as long as three to four buses in a row."

Piper gulped audibly. "Whoa."

But STEAM was on a roll. "Ten feet is also the height of one floor of a standard human dwelling," he reported. "The average Saw will be the size of a one-story house, with a mouth the size of a two-car garage."

"We get it," Gabriel said. "They're big."

"If there's not much other life on Infinity, what do the Saws eat?" Piper asked.

"Rock," Chris said. "Hence all the caves and tunnels." He pulled up a new image, of one of the Sawtooth-made caverns.

"Sounds like they won't be much risk to us, then," Carly commented.

"Oh, I assure you they would not draw a great distinction between stone and human bone," Chris said, a bit too cheerfully.

"Great," Gabriel said, clapping Chris on the shoulder. "Thanks, man. That's comforting."

"They're almost impossible to kill," Chris continued. "They must be stabbed through all six brain nodes"—he pointed to an area on top of the Saw's head and upper back—"before they have time to heal. Even from the worst stab wounds, they regenerate—only angrier. You really don't want to get cornered by one of these." The camera screen panned through the Sawtooth cavern, drawing deeper and deeper into darkness. "Luckily, the tunnel system is quite vast. There is almost always an escape route."

"Looks like it would be easy to get turned around down there," Piper said, staring at the maze on the screen.

"Yes," Chris said.

They waited for him to add, *And here's how we make sure we don't get lost. . . .* But Chris didn't say anything.

"Avoid Saws. Check," Dash said. "Next?"

Chris brought up an image of a winged black horse. The midnight-colored steed reared back on its hind legs and pawed the air, unfurling its silken wings. The creature's eyes glowed white, making it look slightly demonic. Yet, strangely, the whole crew smiled at the sight.

"Oh," Carly exclaimed. "They're awesome."

"Yes, truly awful," Chris said, sounding like he was agreeing with her.

"Are they enemies?" Carly felt suddenly very disappointed. "They look so beautiful."

"Wild, they are neither enemy nor friend," Chris said. "Unpredictable at best. When domesticated, Weavers become somewhat similar to Earth horses. They can be ridden. In fact, that is the best way to explore the Sawtooth caverns."

"So . . . giant eels with scissor jaws, long-tailed stinging cave bats, and flying demon horses?" Gabriel summed up. "All in a day's work."

"At least there are no other people to avoid," Piper said, trying to keep things positive. After all the wacky politics on Aqua Gen, they could use a break from the challenge of dealing with other-planet societies.

"Well . . . ," said Chris.

"Oh, great." Gabriel slapped his forehead. "You always save the best for last."

"The Jackals are a friendly race," Chris added quickly. "If a bit . . . regimented."

"That doesn't sound too good," Carly said.

"But it doesn't sound terrible," Dash added. "If they're friendly, then at least maybe we'll have some locals to show us around."

"Infinity is not their home planet," Chris said. "The Jackals on Infinity are explorers and scientists. Everything is documented and recorded for study."

"Great. So we're about to become an entry in some mad-scientist alien's diary?" Gabriel quipped.

Chris looked puzzled as the others laughed. "Oh, no, I assure you the Jackals are not an angry race," he said. The crew laughed a little harder.

" 'Mad scientist' is kind of a saying," Piper explained. Even though he looked like a human teenager, Chris was an alien through and through.

Chris shrugged and continued. "All that's left is to figure out who's going."

"Gabriel," Dash said. "That tunnel system sounds like it's going to need serious navigation skills."

Gabriel nodded agreement. "I'm on it."

"And Carly," said Piper. "She knows the most about riding horses."

Carly nodded eagerly too. She loved to ride. Some of her favorite memories of home involved going to the countryside, where friends of her family owned stables and a dozen horses.

"Horselike creatures," Chris reminded them. "Not actual horses."

Dash and Piper looked at each other. Usually only a team of three went to the surface. The fourth crew member stayed on board the *Cloud Leopard* with Chris in case of an emergency. They'd broken their rule on Aqua Gen, with nearly devastating consequences.

"I can ride a horse, no problem," Piper said. "It won't be that different from being on my air chair. Or," she added, "I can just air chair my way through the tunnels."

Dash nodded. "Yeah, that makes sense." He hesitated to say it, but between the Saws and the Stingers, it also seemed like there might be a need for Piper's medical skills down on the surface. Much as Dash wanted to go on the adventure—because he always wanted to go—he had been along on all the planet surface trips so far. It was only fair he take a turn staying on the ship.

Dash opened his mouth to confirm who would be going: "Great. So it'll be Gabriel, Carly, and—"

"Actually," Chris said. "I'd like to go along this time."

Piper looked surprised and disappointed, but she took the news gracefully. "Oh," she said. "Well, there's probably not a need for all four of us to go."

Dash was surprised too. Chris always stayed on the ship, at least initially. He had a way of making an entrance onto the planets, when he needed to. "Why do you want to go along this time?"

"I would like to smooth things over with the Jackals." Chris stared at the surface of the table as he spoke.

"I thought you said they were friendly," Piper said. She hoped it didn't sound like she was complaining about being excluded from the mission. Even though she was disappointed, she thought it was perfectly fair to let Chris have a turn. Frankly, Piper was still recovering from all the activity on Aqua Gen. Things had gotten pretty rough for her in the waters there. But she'd never admit it to the others or let it interfere with her work on the rest of the mission. No way.

"We shouldn't have any problems with the Jackals," Chris said.

Carly frowned and glanced at Piper. She wondered if the other girl was thinking the same thing she was: That "having no problems" wasn't exactly the same as being friendly.

"So, that's settled," Dash said. "Piper and I will stay here. We'll be on hand if anything goes wrong down there."

"Don't say it like that," Carly chided. "You'll jinx us."

"Yeah, 'cause that's never happened," Gabriel said. "Everything's gone perfectly so far."

The crew grinned at one another. It felt good to laugh and joke about the seriousness of things to come. It reminded them that, in spite of the danger, they were in this together.

Carly and Gabriel exchanged an extra glance as the crew broke out of their circle. It would be the two of them and Chris? And Dash would stay on the ship? Weird.

The briefing broke up as the crew went their separate ways to prepare. Dash rode the tunnels down to the engine room. The ZRKs zipped industrially up and down the walls. Dash had come to help, but slowly it sank in that, this time, there was not much prep for him to do. He didn't even need to pack a bag or anything. He stood alone there for a moment.

In this room, more than any place else on the ship, the danger and the importance of their mission really hit home. The area was full of sounds as the ship steadied out after leaving Gamma Speed. One portion of the room was occupied by the Element Fuser, the machine that the Voyagers would use to combine the elements once they had all six in hand. The rest of the space was filled by the various smaller ships, vehicles, and watercrafts that the team used to venture out on planet. Some had taken significant damage. And there were empty spaces now too, for the ones the crew had had to leave behind.

Dash breathed deeply, feeling the adrenaline rush still pumping through his veins. His heart was still pounding—why wouldn't it stop? He cared for his crew, but he should feel safe himself now, shouldn't he? Then again, the engine room held the memory of the dangers they had already faced. And it promised—or warned—of more to come.

It was all happening again now.

Gabriel and Carly scurried around gathering the supplies they would need for the on-planet excursion. They each stuffed their backpack with their various tool pouches, work gloves, a basic first-aid kit, some light snacks, and a water bottle. They expected to be down and back within the course of the day, but you never knew what could happen.

Chris seemed less concerned about general preparations, but he took time to carefully advise Gabriel and Carly about the nets he had prepared for the Stinger excursion. They had a pretty neat setup, Carly thought. Each was basically a high-tech butterfly net, with a metal hoop on a long pole that extended at the push of a button, like an umbrella. A big mesh net hung from the hoop. The coolest part was the drawstring lever. One tug of the trigger-like mechanism on the pole and the mouth of the net drew closed.

"So, we'll fly into the caverns on Weavers and catch the Stingers with these nets?" Gabriel said. He clicked open his pole and waved the net around like a flag. It was lightweight and easy to maneuver. "This is going to be awesome!"

Carly ducked as he swung it a little too close to her head. "Hey," she called. "You're collecting Stingers, not crewmates."

"I was nowhere near you," he said. "Chicken."

Carly scoffed. "Who you calling chicken, turkey?" She extended her own net, and they play-jousted for a minute. Carly tried to brush off the comment Gabriel had made. She knew he meant it as a joke. But it hit home, because Carly sometimes secretly felt like a chicken. She tried to act brave, but the idea of stepping off the *Cloud Leopard* scared her every time. She'd stayed on the ship for the first two planet missions, partly out of fear. She'd proved herself capable on Aqua Gen, for sure, but the old fears still lingered sometimes.

"Take that!" Gabriel whacked her lightly with his net. Carly groaned in mock agony and staggered to the side.

Dash strode into the chamber right then. "Stop messing around. We don't have time to waste." His voice was stiff. He sounded almost angry.

"Chill out, bro," Gabriel said. He folded the net and hooked it into place on his backpack. "We're going." When he shouldered the pack, the net hung neatly in place behind him.

Carly hugged Dash. "See you soon," she promised. She had learned that she wasn't the only one who got scared and anxious. Her friends also needed to blow off steam sometimes before the big missions. Everyone got nervous and stressed and showed it in different ways. Gabriel's way was goofing off a bit. Dash's way was to get all tight and start ordering people around.

Dash nodded as she pulled away. "Good luck down there."

"Can't leave without the gifts," Chris said, returning to the chamber. "Jackals are big on ceremony."

As if on cue, a small fleet of ZRKs flew in carrying

the treats. They had decided upon large packages of tea and cookies as hospitality offerings. The ZRKs carried a textbook-sized wooden box of hibiscus tea and about a dozen shrink-wrapped tubes of freshly baked chocolate-chip cookies.

"Brilliant," Gabriel said, reaching for the cookies. He tucked them away as Carly stuffed the tea box into her own backpack.

They all headed through the engine room to the *Cloud Cat* docking bay. Carly, Gabriel, and Chris climbed into the *Cloud Cat,* the smaller landing craft that would fly them down to the planet's surface.

Carly swallowed down the nuggets of fear in her throat. She wasn't going to chicken out. Not this time.

Chris buckled himself into his chair with his normal expression—a slightly secretive smile—in place.

Gabriel took the controls and fired up the engine. The cargo doors opened, and the *Cloud Cat* eased into the atmosphere.

Gabriel grinned as the *Cloud Cat* swooped down through the cloudless sky. "To Infinity, and be—"

"Don't say it," Carly interrupted, laughing.

"Beyond!"

5

Behind the *Cloud Leopard*, as close and as looming as a shadow, a second spaceship steamed through the night at Gamma Speed. It too slowed as it approached the planet Infinity. An arrival announcement echoed through the bridge of the *Light Blade*, but no one was around to hear it. The crew had all gathered downstairs in the training center.

The room looked remarkably similar to the *Cloud Leopard*'s training area, with pads on the floors, and athletic equipment and training supplies scattered around the wide-open space. At the moment, the entire crew of the *Light Blade* was gathered around a structure somewhat resembling a mechanical bull.

Siena Moretti's fingers grew slick with sweat as she clung to the reins. She struggled to stay on board the metal creature as it dipped and swerved. Finally it tilted so far to the right that she slid off the saddle and onto the mat.

Anna Turner clicked off the stopwatch. "That was nearly two minutes."

"Best time so far," Niko Rodriguez chimed in. "My record was ninety-nine seconds."

"You might've beaten him, Siena," Ravi Chavan said, reaching down to help her up off the mat. "But that record won't stand for long. My turn again."

As with most things on the *Light Blade*, the Weaver-riding training had turned into a competition.

"I hope we'll be able to stay on longer than that on the real Weavers," Siena commented. It wasn't like they were going to be contestants in a rodeo. Two minutes was a pretty brief ride.

Anna waved her hand. "Yeah, sure. This is training. It's extra hard on purpose so we can really see who are the best riders."

"So far that's Siena and Niko," Colin said. Colin was the *Light Blade*'s resident alien—a clone of the alien Chris, who was traveling on the *Cloud Leopard.* An icier, more emotionless clone.

"Yeah," Anna agreed. "They're definitely going down to the surface."

Siena and Niko smiled at each other.

"It's between you and me, boss," Ravi taunted the Omega crew leader as he climbed aboard the training horse. "Let me show you all how it's done."

The metal horse began to buck and twist. Thirty

seconds later, the machine sent Ravi sprawling onto the mat. He landed flat on his back with a loud *OOF*.

"Dang," Ravi said, grinning sheepishly up at the others. "That one doesn't count."

Everyone groaned. Anna clapped slowly. "Congratulations, Ravi. With a performance like that, you're clearly a good fit for the mission."

"Ha-ha," Ravi said, jumping to his feet. "I know, I know. You want to go."

Anna glanced at Colin. "Actually, I think you should go ahead."

"Really?" Ravi asked. "How come?"

"Uh, there are other skills that will be needed for the mission," Anna explained quickly. "It's not all about riding."

Siena was surprised at that. Anna always wanted to go on every planet mission. Something about it didn't add up. What had changed?

"Great. Let's go get ready," Ravi said quickly, wanting to act before Anna could change her mind. The crew filed out of the training room, headed for their quarters. Siena glanced over her shoulder at Anna, bringing up the rear. She was smiling slightly.

There were always tricks and games afoot among the *Light Blade* crew. Siena had grown pretty tired of it actually. She didn't feel like she could relax, even on board the ship, among her crewmates.

The *Light Blade*'s whole mission was a game really. The Omega crew had been sent after the Alphas in secret, by Commander Shawn Phillips's father, Ike Phillips. The kids had become pawns in an interstellar game of chess between father and son. Which team would capture all the elements, restore energy to Earth, and reap the glory?

So far, at least as far as Siena could tell, there weren't really any winners in this particular game. But that didn't stop everyone from playing.

Anna wasn't the only one with a competitive edge. Niko and Ravi seemed not to mind the cutthroat energy around here. They fed into it. Siena was tired of feeling like she had to work against everyone. They were supposed to be a team. They weren't in training anymore, needing to prove themselves to each other or to the mission command staff. Now was a time to band together.

Not for the first time, Siena wondered what life aboard the *Cloud Leopard* would be like. She imagined it quite different than the *Light Blade*. The *Cloud Leopard* crew seemed always to be laughing together, even in the face of danger. It was clear they always had each other's backs. No matter what.

Sometimes, when Anna and the others got into their competitive mode, Siena wanted to jump ship. Literally. Would the *Cloud Leopard* crew take her in? The traitorous thought rolled around in her head more often than she cared to admit.

It was terrible to think that way. She knew it. The guilt swamped her as she packed her kit alongside the guys. They gathered in the launch pad to load the *Clipper,* the *Light Blade*'s shuttle. It would have them on the planet's surface in a matter of minutes.

"The *Cloud Cat* is away," Colin reported, entering the chamber. "They've sent Gabriel, Carly, and Chris, surprisingly. It's actually good, because—"

"Wait a minute," Anna said sharply. "Let's not discuss them right now."

Colin smiled icily. He did not like being told what to do. That should never be forgotten.

But he stood quietly as the surface crew packed into the shuttle. Siena, Ravi, and Niko buckled up inside, then the *Clipper* slid out of the cargo bay doors.

"Okay," Anna said. "Now that they're off, we can talk freely about the Alpha team."

"Let's go to the flight deck," Colin said. "There's something I'd like to show you."

6

The *Cloud Cat* skimmed the surface of Infinity. Gabriel, Carly, and Chris looked out the windows and studied the rocky terrain in awe.

"No wonder nothing survives on the surface," Carly said. "It's completely barren." There wasn't so much as a blade of grass or a river in sight. The smooth rock shone gray, awash in predawn light. The view created a somber mood in the landing craft.

In the distance, light glinted off the corner of something metal looming up on the horizon.

"Set it down over there," Chris said. "That's the Jackal compound."

Gabriel brought the *Cloud Cat* to a smooth stop on the flattest stretch of rock he could find.

"This may be our last chance to communicate with the *Cloud Leopard*," Chris informed them. "Once we're underground, the rock will most likely block our signal."

"At least they'll see we've landed safely," Carly said. "We'll get in touch later if we can."

They exited the landing craft one by one, and slowly made their way toward the compound's entrance. Very slowly. It felt like their feet were weighed down.

"Is it me, or is it harder to move than it should be?" Gabriel asked. He felt kind of like he was walking through water.

"Oh, right. This is the gravity issue I mentioned," Chris said. "The planet's core is very dense. It's the gravity."

"Seriously," Carly said. "It's kind of a workout." She tried to jump, but her feet barely left the ground.

Gabriel tried it too. "That's totally freaky," he said. He was used to being quick on his feet.

It wasn't too bad once they got used to it. By the time they reached the tall metal doors, they barely noticed the bit of extra energy it took to walk.

Chris knocked on the door. The thick metal sheet thumped and rattled as he pounded.

"I'm sure they've seen us by now," he commented, pointing up at a massive fish-eye lens mounted on the upper edge of the door frame. Jackal technology.

They waited.

And waited.

Nothing happened.

Carly glanced around, slightly nervous. Even though there was no specific threat on the surface of Infinity, she wanted to remain alert. On their last mission, the danger started the moment they set down on a planet.

Chris pounded on the door again.

Nothing.

"Very strange," he said.

Gabriel shrugged. "We can greet the Jackals later. How do we get to the caves?"

"There are many entrances, but the most direct route is through their outpost," Chris answered. "They've built access tunnels. And mapped the interior."

Gabriel reached for the door handle. He twisted the knob, and the door swung open inward, revealing a dark foyer.

"We can't enter without permission," Chris protested. "That definitely goes against Jackal hospitality protocol."

"It's open," Carly said. "So it's not like we're breaking and entering."

"It should be locked," Chris murmured. "This is very strange indeed."

"We need those maps," Gabriel insisted. "We're on a schedule here."

"We don't have a choice," Carly agreed. She followed Gabriel into the dim space.

As they stepped inside, a string of bulbous orange lights illuminated the space. They were like the strings of bulbs people put on their roofs around the holidays, only much bigger. The size of gallon milk jugs.

The foyer narrowed to a corridor that wound slightly downhill. The lights along each row came on one by one, disappearing around the bend at the bottom of the slope.

Chris took the lead, apparently coming around to agree that they had to proceed. "I'm not sure this is best," he said as he walked. "But, considering our time limitations. . . ." His voice trailed off.

The corridor ended in a large living room. The space was full of institutional furniture, like you might find in a dentist's waiting room. Rows of slightly cushioned chairs with upholstery that looked like leather, separated by low coffee tables. More of the bulbous orange lamps stuck out of the tables like crystal balls or neon pumpkins. The whole place had a warm, fiery glow.

Gabriel touched the back of one of the chairs. It was slick, gray-green, and vaguely familiar. "Is it me, or does that look like . . . ?"

Chris nodded. "Sawtooth skin. Good for all-weather clothing and upholstery. Very durable."

Carly and Gabriel exchanged a glance. Skinning Saws didn't sound like anyone's idea of fun.

Several dark corridors snaked away from the central waiting room. As soon as Carly walked toward the mouth of one hall, it lit up. Like the entryway, the corridor was lined with strings of colored lights on both sides. Instead of being all orange, it was only orange on the left. The string of lights on the right hand side was all green.

Gabriel walked toward a different hallway, and that one lit up orange and blue. It turned out that the lights in each hallway had orange, plus a different color. Green. Blue. White. Brown. Red.

"It's for navigation," Chris explained. "The left-hand lights stand for the room you are coming from. The right-hand lights tell you which room you're going to."

"That's smart." Carly had a feeling they were only starting to be impressed by the Jackals' technology.

"Jackals are an advanced race," Chris said. "The team on Infinity is primarily explorers and research scientists. Everything is systematized." He glanced around. "If I recall correctly, green leads to the research division. They must be down there working."

"Maybe that's why they didn't hear us knock," Carly suggested.

They followed the green lights. The corridor led to a cluster of glass-walled laboratories.

Dozens of labs.

None were occupied.

In fact, none looked like they had been occupied for a very long time.

The first lab they entered contained a lot of complicated-looking machinery. There were shelves of test tubes, graduated cylinders, and what looked like neon Tupperware. Lights glowed on some of the machines, but none emitted any sound. Not even the barest hum of a running refrigerator.

Gabriel ran his finger over the countertop and picked up a layer of dust. He wiped it quickly on his pants, and shivered slightly. This eerie outpost, with its abandoned labs, totally skeeved him out.

"They've gone," Chris said, sounding disappointed. "When they didn't answer the door, I knew something wasn't right."

"They left all their stuff, it looks like," Gabriel said. He picked up an empty canister that might have once held crayons. The opaque plastic walls appeared smudged with colorful wax. He shook it upside down, as if something invisible could fall out. Nothing but a puff of dust emerged.

"Let's keep looking," Carly said. "Maybe we'll still find something we can use."

The next lab appeared to be devoted to the study of Stingers. One wall had a grid of small and medium-sized animal cages, like you might find full of mice or birds in a biology lab back on Earth. They were empty.

The wall held a series of anatomical pictures of Stingers: front view, side views, top view, belly view. A close-up on the crazy-looking barbed tail. Framed beside it was a real live skeleton under glass. And beside that, a detailed artist's rendering of the Stinger's internal organs.

Gabriel took a close look at the skeleton. "So this is what we're up against." He grinned. "Doesn't look so terrible."

"Famous last words," Carly muttered.

Carly examined a rack of what appeared to be surgical tools—knives and scalpels, scissors and forceps, mallets and straight pins, tweezers and clamps of all shapes and sizes. "Yikes," she said. "You could do a lot of damage with this arsenal."

Gabriel noticed a small jar of what looked like BBs resting on the countertop. "Hey, look!" he said. "Aren't these the spores we need?"

Chris glanced at the jar. "Yeah, looks like it," he said. "But that is not nearly enough. We need a thousand, remember?"

The jar contained maybe twenty. Gabriel shook it, and the spores rattled like a maraca. "That's music to my ears," he said. "Twenty down, only nine thousand, nine hundred, and eighty to go!"

Carly rolled her eyes. "Woo-hoo. We really put

a dent in the spore count just now." She laughed, raising her fists in a pretend celebration. "But seriously," she added, "maybe we should poke around and look for some more." She started opening cabinets. It made sense to stay positive, but she knew there was no chance they could avoid facing down the live Stingers.

"I doubt these will be fresh enough," Chris warned. "The toxin's potency will have faded over time."

"Better safe than sorry." Jar in hand, Gabriel swung his backpack off and began to unzip it.

"No," Chris said sharply. "We cannot take that without permission."

Gabriel blew the layer of dust off the lid and popped the jar into his backpack anyway. "The place is deserted. What's the big deal?"

A slight mechanical sound whirred from somewhere above and behind them.

Carly spun around.

The fish-eye camera mounted high in one corner traced a slow arc within its frame. Carly looked at it for a moment, wondering if someone was looking back at her.

"This place gives me the creeps," Gabriel said. He led the way back into the hall. "Let's get on with it. How do we find these Sawtooth tunnels?"

"Listen," Carly said. A soft whinnying sound

carried through the hallways from someplace out of sight. "Do you hear that?"

Gabriel cocked his head and listened. "Yeah, what is it?"

"Sounds like Weavers, maybe," Carly mused. "Come on. I can't wait to see them." The whinnying drew her like a beacon of light amid the darkness. It sounded so familiar, so warm.

"It is bad enough that we are in their space without proper admittance," Chris said. His usually monotone voice betrayed a hint of nervousness. "We cannot take too many liberties."

"We have a job to do," Gabriel said. "And no one's here."

With Carly leading the way, they followed the sound. This corridor was lined with green and black lights. Before long, they found themselves at the edge of a deep, high-ceilinged cavern. The entrance to the large open space was protected by a narrow gate of two horizontal bars.

"A quick look will not hurt anything," Chris conceded. "Since we're already this far inside. But we cannot borrow them without permission." Chris unclasped the gate latch at one side and swung it open.

Carly and Gabriel stepped past him into the Weaver enclosure. The black animals roamed free in their allotted space. Two strolled around the stony pasture, while the other four dipped and swirled in the air, stretching their wings.

"Whoa," Gabriel blurted out. "They really are like horses with wings. Crazy."

The Weavers looked quite *real* to him, like a thing that could have been found back on Earth, unlike so many of the beings they'd encountered. And yet, they were so clearly "other."

They smelled musky and dark—if a thing could smell dark—and they radiated calmness and grace. One of the Weavers cantered straight toward Carly. It pressed its damp muzzle against her shoulder, sniffing curiously. She reached up and stroked its silken black mane. The strands felt liquid smooth, like passing her hand through a flowing stream of water.

"Hey, you," she whispered. "How are you? Nice to meet you."

The Weaver whinnied, sounding so much like an Earth horse that Carly grew homesick. She reached up and hugged the creature's sinewy neck, and the Weaver stood still and allowed it. If she closed her eyes, she could imagine she was standing in a grassy field surrounded by lush Japanese countryside. The Weaver breathed a gentle gust from his nose, and Carly swore she smelled her mother's cooking on the breeze. This is the one she would ride, Carly decided then and there.

Gabriel looked around the edges of the pen.

A row of six saddles hung on one wall. Helmets, reins, bits, crops, and other riding gear rested on a set of shelves. Beside that hung a rack of wicked-looking swords.

"Yikes," Gabriel said, upon seeing those long swords. These were definitely not dulled and blunted for sparring. They were the real deal, and much longer than the practice pair up on the ship. Each saddle had two fat sword scabbards, one on each side. "Maybe the Jackals sword-fight two-handed. That's nuts."

He backed away from the arsenal slowly. He headed over toward Carly and the Weavers. For Gabriel, the horselike creatures felt even less familiar than the crazy swords. He had ridden once, a long time ago, but . . . Oh, boy.

He stood still as a statue as one of the Weavers began to nudge and sniff him. It was so tall. So alive.

A few feet away, Carly was all nuzzled up against her Weaver, stroking its mane.

Nope. I'm not hugging you, dude, Gabriel thought. He tentatively patted the Weaver's nose. The Weaver snuffled, casting a tiny wind around his fingers. Gabriel flinched.

Navigation was his thing. That's why he was here. The reality of the whole "riding a horse" thing . . . He swallowed hard. He sort of hadn't given it much thought up until now.

He hoped the Weavers turned out to be as easy to steer as a go-cart or the *Cloud Cat*. He could drive pretty much anything that didn't have a mind of its own. As the Weaver gazed upon him with deep, liquid eyes, Gabriel knew this adventure was going to be a bit different.

"We're going to have to borrow them, permission or not," Carly commented. "Unless there's something you're not telling us about the Jackals, Chris, in which case, now would be a good time to clue us in," she added, turning around.

But Chris was nowhere to be seen.

7

Far on the other side of Infinity, a second small landing craft skimmed the rocky surface.

"Set down over there," Siena determined. She pointed toward a craggy mountain range jutting up against the sky in the distance. She consulted the hand-drawn sketch of the planet's surface that Colin had given them.

"At the base of those hills, right?" Ravi confirmed.

"Right."

"Is there going to be a door or something?" Niko wondered.

"Probably just a hole in the ground," Ravi said. "I'll try not to set the ship down right in it."

"Yeah, let's avoid getting stuck in a pothole," Siena said.

Silence returned to the *Clipper* landing craft. Premission tension. Everyone had their game face on.

There were plenty of other entrances to the caves that didn't require going through the Jackal compound. Colin's map led to one of them.

From there, they'd have to record their progress through the tunnels carefully so they could find their way back out. Maps were useless underground, Colin had insisted, since the tunnels changed so often.

That's why they could comfortably avoid the Jackals—and any difficult negotiations that might ensue. "Leave the diplomacy to the Alphas," Colin had said with a hint of a sneer. "They're all into teamwork, so there's no chance they'll dodge the Jackals. It'll slow them down. Meanwhile, we'll be in and out and waiting for them."

"The terrain is not as flat as I expected," Ravi said. The landing craft skimmed along the textured landscape, approaching the mountain. "This might be a rocky landing."

"No pun intended," Niko grumbled good-naturedly. Siena laughed.

Ravi set the craft down with a bit of a jolt.

"Are we there yet?" Niko joked as the ship's frame rocked and settled.

They trudged with heavy legs to the edge of the cave entrance. From the surface, it looked less like a cave and more like a gaping pit in the planet's surface.

The hole was deep. A pitch-black funnel into the depths of Infinity. Its edges were raw and jagged. Gray-brown dust came away in Siena's fingers as she ran her hand along the rim.

The trio set up their climbing ropes, securing them to a large rock near the mouth of the hole. They would rappel down into the cave one at a time.

"Who's first?" Siena asked.

"I landed us here," Ravi said. "You two duke it out."

"I'll go last," Siena suggested. "I'm the best at handling the climbing equipment."

They turned to Niko, who grinned broadly. "Like I was gonna let either of you beat me in there."

Ravi took hold of Niko's safety rope to belay. Just in case.

Siena stood by the rock, triple- and quadruple-checking the apparatus to make sure it was well in place. They didn't know how deep the tunnel was, so Niko would rappel down a few feet at a time until he found bottom.

"Here goes nothing," Niko said. He tested the rope's tautness against the rock one last time, then launched himself into the crater. His feet bounced against the side wall as he hopped downward, loosening and tightening his clamp on the rope with each jump. Soon he had descended out of sight.

Ravi held Niko's safety rope more loosely than Siena would have preferred. Granted, it was also tied to the giant rock, but still. She was going third for a reason. She would rather trust the rock.

"This is totally creepy," Niko's voice echoed out of the hole.

Siena checked the depth counter, which was tracking Niko's descent based on a locator chip in his harness. "Fifty feet."

"I can't see a dang thing," Niko complained. "Just walls."

"Seventy-five feet."

"It's pretty dry down here. And cool."

"Those chills are from fright," Ravi called in a taunting voice. "Is somebody a little scared of the dark?"

"Shut up," Niko called back. "You'll be crying for your mama when it's your turn."

Siena watched Ravi's hands tighten around the rope, then loosen again. "One hundred feet."

"We only dropped two hundred feet of rope in there, right?"

"Yeah," Siena said. "If it's farther than that, then we have to try a different hole."

"It wasn't supposed to be this deep," Ravi said.

"Tunnels change," Siena reminded him. She glanced at the counter showing Niko's progress. "One hundred thirty feet."

They stood in silence and stared down into the hole. The silence was remarkable. It was a far cry from what they were used to. No plants or animals to make noise. Barely a breeze. Too silent.

"He stopped talking," Ravi noticed.

"Or we stopped hearing him?" Siena suggested hopefully.

The climbing rope began to tremble and bob.

"Oh no." She barely breathed it.

Ravi tightened up on the safety line . . . which turned slack in his hands. He drew it up quickly, yard by yard, until a frayed end appeared in his hand. He turned to Siena, alarmed. "Do you think he got eaten?"

The climbing rope jerked more distinctly. Again. And again.

"Wait, he's pulling on the rope," Siena realized, relieved. "He's found bottom." The counter had stopped. "One hundred and forty-five feet." Siena reset the counter to track the depth of Ravi's harness instead of Niko's.

"Okay, here I go," Ravi said. He tightened the safety rope against the rock, then clipped his own harness to it and to the main climbing rope. He winked at Siena. "See ya soon."

Alone on the surface of Infinity, the silence felt even more profound.

The place was neither desert, nor mountain, nor

plain. Only rock and dust and stillness. It was hard to even believe in the dangers that lay below while she was surrounded by such utter lifelessness. It was especially odd to realize that at the moment she might be the sole living thing on the surface of an entire planet.

When it was Siena's turn, she sighed as she lowered herself into the hole. A few calm minutes, without tension and wisecracking, was a lot lately. It had felt strange, but good.

One hundred and forty-five feet below the surface, the three Omegas regrouped and ventured into the tunnels. The wide, dark cavern was made only a little less dark by their flashlights, but if Colin was correct, there should be Stingers found easily nearby.

The Omega crew didn't need any help from the Jackals. They could do it all on their own.

It was better this way.

They'd get in and out, no problem, Colin had assured them. Quick and clean and, hopefully, unnoticed.

8

"**Where did Chris** go?" Carly asked. The Weaver cavern seemed bigger and stranger all of a sudden.

Gabriel shrugged. "We'd better find him."

They wandered up the hallway, back in the direction they had come. The empty labs seemed even eerier now, if possible. Other hallways spun off in many directions. Chris could have gone anywhere.

"He can't have just vanished," Gabriel said.

"Or so you think," Carly said, trying to make her voice sound mysterious. It wasn't hard in these surroundings. "Maybe he's been concealing alien teleporting technology from us all this time."

"Ha," Gabriel said. "You think he's going to reappear, in a tuxedo or something?" He laughed and made jazz hands, shaking his palms out to the sides. "Surprise!"

Carly laughed too. It felt like they needed to

fill the silence. The quiet in the labs was too eerie otherwise.

It was extra odd being just the two of them. *Gabriel Parker and Carly Diamond, alone in the vastness of Infinity . . .* The words echoed in her head like a movie-trailer voice-over.

Carly took the opportunity to contact the *Cloud Leopard.* She raised her MTB and tried to radio Dash and Piper.

No luck. The connection failed to produce even static.

Chris had been right—the rock blocked all radio signals to the surface. Plus, the part of the Jackal outpost that was on the surface must have been relatively small. They were definitely deep underground now. The walls here appeared to have been carved straight out of the stone.

"Hey, look at this," Carly exclaimed. She entered one of the labs they hadn't explored yet. It was mostly empty, except for a battered-looking metal safe the size of a mini refrigerator.

The small safe looked like it had been dropped from a great height. It was all crinkled and crushed, like an empty juice box. The smashed metal door had rings for a padlock, but there wasn't one. It didn't appear to be locked—just so damaged that it had become impossible to open.

Gabriel tugged on the door. It didn't budge.

Carly examined the safe from all sides. "There's writing over here." She tapped the MTB on her wrist and brought up their translation program. The crew had a special translator device, but as a safety precaution, Chris had downloaded the program to their MTBs too.

"It translates to 'tunnel navigation system,'" she reported. "Approximately."

Gabriel grinned, excited. "Wait . . . it says 'approximately'?" he asked. "Why would you want to navigate approximately?"

"I think it means it's an approximate translation."

"Oh. That's even weirder." Gabriel took off his backpack and rummaged inside it for a minute. He pulled out a small black pouch.

Carly knocked on the safe's metal walls, as if hoping someone might open it from the inside. "We have to open it," she insisted. "Maybe we can pry the door loose with a screwdriver?"

"Yeah, I have one right in here—" Gabriel unzipped the black pouch. "Yahh!" he cried, jumping back in surprise. His padded Simu Suit loomed over him like a ghost.

Carly laughed at his stunned expression. "Why'd you even bring that?"

"I didn't mean to," Gabriel said. "I thought it was my tool pouch. Shoot. I must have picked up the wrong one when I was packing." They were both small black zippered pouches. He could easily see how he'd made the mistake.

"Oh," Carly said. "So we don't actually have your tool pouch with us?"

Gabriel rummaged in his bag. "I guess not. Sorry."

"It's not a big deal," Carly said. "This place is pretty well stocked. We can probably find any tools we need around here." She scanned the shelves while Gabriel set about refolding the Simu Suit. He squished the foam flatter and flatter and zipped it back into place. He returned the pouch to his backpack, still feeling kind of embarrassed over the confusion.

Carly pulled a scraper from the bottom of a shelf. It had a flat metal head about two inches wide and a thicker blue plastic handle. "Here—why don't we try this?"

"That works." Gabriel helped Carly position the lip of the scraper in the space along the edge of the safe door. He pushed all of his weight against it.

The door inched open.

The contents of the safe were . . . utterly disappointing.

"It's paint." Carly said. Several stacks of fist-sized canisters. Except they were all the same pale yellow color. Barely yellow, more like a saltine cracker. Each can had a pair of hooks looping off the rim, like quotation marks. Or fangs. A stack of clean brushes accompanied them.

"Well, that was anticlimactic," Gabriel added dryly.

"I guess they've repurposed this safe." Carly poked at the lid of the paint can. "And it's not even a good color."

Gabriel rolled his eyes jokingly. "Haven't you heard? Neon pale is the new black."

"Like I'm ever going to trust your fashion sense," Carly quipped.

He grabbed three cans and started juggling them, only to watch them crash onto the floor and flop in all directions. "Whoa, that is some heavy paint," he said.

"Extra gravity, remember?" Carly reminded him.

"Right." Gabriel bent down and picked a can up by the fangs. He twirled it around his finger. It was heavier than swinging a ceramic mug.

"Let's go," Carly said. "We have to find Chris." She went into the hall. A minute later, Gabriel joined her. He was still messing around in his bag.

"Careful," Carly warned. "You got any other surprises in there?"

Gabriel grinned. "I just might."

They walked past additional labs. Gabriel looked in the door of each, in case anything caught his eye. He felt torn between the creepy fun of exploring the labs, and the need to find Chris and get on with the mission. There might be other useful things to find, but they had a job to do here too.

The corridor dead-ended in a T. The new hallway was wider than the others had been. There was a row of red bulbs mounted high on the far wall, but that was it. Several appeared shattered.

"Which way now?" Carly asked.

"I guess they stopped putting in lighting at some point," Gabriel said. He flicked on his flashlight and pointed it both ways down the dark hall. Then he shrugged. "This way."

They turned left and made their way down the corridor. The sound of their footsteps became echo-ey. Beside them, the row of red lights blinked three times, then went out.

"Huh," Gabriel said. "Does this feel right to you?"

"Maybe they're on a timer." Carly pulled out her flashlight too. The dual beams made it somewhat easier to see the path in front of them.

"Oh, look!" Carly said. She hurried through the swath of light toward the thing that had caught her eye. "A flower. Isn't it pretty?"

She bent to examine it. It was hard to tell in the darkness what color it was. Lavender, she thought, or something close. It had a broad flat face, sort of like a daisy, but with thick, round petals that felt full, like aloe leaves. It grew from a flexible, four-stranded stem that curved out of a moss-lined crack in the wall.

When Carly reached down and touched the stem, she wasn't intending to pluck the flower. The stem strands severed seemingly of their own accord. They coiled around her index finger and thumb, gripping like a baby's fist.

"Cool," Gabriel said.

"Why is it growing indoors?" Carly wondered.

"Um, it's not . . . ," Gabriel said, coming up closer behind her. He swept the flashlight over the wall she was crouched near. It wasn't smooth, as if cut by man-made tools. It was made of jagged stone.

The realization dawned slowly. "We're not in the Jackal building anymore," Carly said. This tunnel was more than three times as tall as they were—at least fifteen feet high—and just about that wide. Like a circle. A circle chewed out by giant stone-cutting teeth.

"These are the Sawtooth caves," Gabriel said. He shone the flashlight back the way they had come. All jagged stone, as far as they could see.

"When did it change?" Carly said. "Why didn't we notice?" As she spoke, the flower tendrils coiled snugly, tucking deeper into the spaces between her fingers.

"I don't know. The difference must be subtle at

first," Gabriel said. "We were focused on finding Chris."

"Let's get back. We should find him before we go farther," Carly said.

Gabriel agreed. "We need the maps."

"And the Weavers."

They started walking back the way they had come. The hallway seemed much longer and darker now.

Carly was the first to hear the scraping sound. "Did you hear that?"

"It's nothing," Gabriel said. "Let's just get back to the Jackal compound."

The scraping sound grew louder. Or . . . closer.

It was the shushing of leathery skin on stone. "Something's coming," Carly said.

Whatever Gabriel was going to say in response was drowned out by the grind of stone-cutting jaws. A massive Sawtooth Land Eel slid around the corner in front of them, gnashing and slathering.

9

Dash and Piper stuck close to the *Cloud Leopard* flight deck, waiting for communication from their crew down on Infinity.

So far, total radio silence.

Dash stood at the screen and gazed out at the desolate landscape. The lifelessness of the place had a certain beauty. The gray rocks shone in the pale light of the nearest star. The planet had a rainy-day gloom about it that lifted gradually as the starlight peeked over the horizon.

A sunrise in a distant world.

It reminded Dash of a sunrise in the desert, when he and his mom and sister had traveled to the Grand Canyon when he was little. Then, and now, the view made him feel small, but also connected to something bigger than himself. The earth, the air, the universe. Something.

His mom had held his hand that day, to keep him from getting too close to the canyon edge. Now he flexed his empty fingers and fought against the warm memory of that vacation long ago.

It was strange to think of himself so far from home. He didn't want to dwell on those thoughts. He couldn't afford to let his mind slip into sadness, nostalgia, or fear. If he ever wanted to make it home again, he had to stay ready and keep the crew on task.

Dash turned away from the view screen.

"They should be checking in with us," he said.

"Give it time," Piper answered. "It hasn't been that long, really. We don't know what might be going on down there."

"Yeah, that's what I'm worried about," Dash informed her.

Piper nodded. "I'm sure they'll radio in when they can. Or when they need to." The last bit carried an ominous echo.

"No news is good news?" Dash said wryly, trying for a positive spin.

Piper shrugged. "Something like that."

Dash turned back to the large screen. Clear sky. The stillness of rock. "Since when has a planet brought us good news?" he mused. Feelings of worry churned around in his belly.

"They're underground, remember?" Piper said. "Maybe there's just no signal."

Maybe. Yet the nagging feeling in Dash's gut

still gnawed at him. "Something doesn't feel right," he said. "I should be down there with them."

Or me, Piper thought, although she knew Dash was speaking out of frustration. "Sometimes being part of the team means watching and waiting," she said. "This is what they need from us right now."

"Yeah." Dash's tone was flat, the word but a short puff of breath.

Piper was familiar with the frustration of being left behind, and the desire to plunge in and help the team. Such impulsiveness had gotten the best of her on the last planet. This time, she was prepared to stay calm and levelheaded.

Dash came away from the screen, still with a troubled look on his face. He plopped into the seat closest to Piper's air chair. "Do you think Chris told us everything?"

Piper lowered her gaze. Her lips parted as her mind warred between speaking the truth and keeping the peace. "No, actually, I don't."

The Saw was headed straight toward Carly and Gabriel, and it was blocking the mouth of the tunnel that led back into the Jackal compound. The eel was so large that their flashlight beams couldn't illuminate its whole face. Not that they wanted to see its whole face.

"Run!" Carly grabbed Gabriel's arm as they spun around and dashed deeper into the dark. The Saw chomped and slithered after them.

They ran past the place where Carly had discovered the flower. Soon the cave tunnel split into a Y. They stopped running, uncertain.

"Which way?" Gabriel blurted out. "I haven't studied the maps yet."

Carly looked back over her shoulder. As frightening and deadly as the thing behind them was, it wasn't moving all that fast. Outrunning it might not really be their biggest problem.

"We can't get lost in here," Carly said. "If we get mixed up, we might never get back."

"It's coming," Gabriel said.

They couldn't turn around. There would be no way to get past the Saw. Its massive body nearly filled the width of the tunnel. And it was close now.

"Pick a lane!" Carly cried. "You're the navigator."

Gabriel darted into the right-hand arm of the tunnel. "If we turn right at every fork going in, then we'll know to always turn left on the way back."

Carly followed. "Will that work?"

Gabriel's voice echoed in the widening tunnel. "I hope so."

The Saw took the right-hand turn too.

"Dang," Gabriel said. "That was some luck."

"It's like flipping a coin," Carly said. "It has to come up in our favor eventually."

The next right they came to was a smaller side tunnel that must have led to another set of caves. It was pitch-black but for the small beads of their flashlights. It didn't seem possible that the dark could get any darker, and yet it did. Their lights appeared to shine less and less distance ahead of them.

"No," Gabriel said, stopping suddenly. Carly bumped into him from behind.

"Go, go," she urged him.

"Uh . . ." Gabriel had his hand stretched out in front of him, pressing against a wall of stone. The tunnel was a dead end. The "always turn right" plan had seemed smart a minute ago. Now Gabriel feared he had signed their death warrant.

The Saw had already reached the crossroads behind them. No going back.

"Now what?" Carly asked.

"Hope it doesn't turn?" Gabriel offered.

"Great."

They inched backward into the space and waited. There was nothing else to do. They had a fifty-fifty shot of being eaten alive.

The Saw made the right turn, which was, in this case, entirely the wrong turn.

Carly's stomach practically dropped into her shoes.

They were dead.

They'd failed.

The mission was over.

"I'm sorry," Gabriel said. Over and over he said it, grasping desperately at the stones as if feeling for some possible exit to materialize. "I'm so sorry, Carly."

Carly felt the strange flower move against her finger. She shone her flashlight at it. If she was going to die, at least she could take one last look at something pretty. The flower tendrils tightened around her finger. She wasn't imagining it, was she? They pulled her arm to the side. Repeatedly. Insistently. Tugging.

"Um, there's something . . ." She relaxed her hand and let the flower take over. Her arm raised in front of her as if of its own accord. She followed the tugging sensation. The flower was pulling her forward in the tunnel—back toward the Saw!

It took all the courage Carly had to follow it. She felt with her hand along the stone wall until . . . the wall wasn't there anymore. Carly nearly stumbled as her hand slid into a gap in the stone. It was barely a foot wide, but deeper than her arm was long. A fissure in the rock.

"Gabe, get over here," Carly shouted. She waved

her flashlight back toward him. He appeared at her side as she pressed herself into the gap. Gabriel smashed himself in behind her.

"Think thin," Carly whispered.

Up close, the Saw's gnashing teeth looked like icicles of steel. The Saw bit and snapped at the edges of the tunnel, widening the walls as it moved through. Its cool breath smelled like a cloud of construction-site dust.

"Whoa!" Gabriel yelped as it chewed the rocks right beside his shoulder.

The Saw's tapered tail slithered past their hiding spot. It chewed its way forward. Soon the tunnel would no longer be a dead end. This was an exact example of how navigation could be impossible down here, Gabriel realized. How many Saws were out there, chewing and changing the tunnels right this minute? Any maps the Jackals had were bound to be outdated within minutes.

Carly and Gabriel squeezed out of the crevice. "Two left turns," Gabriel recalled. They darted through the tunnels. Everything looked different, coming from the other way. The tunnel actually *was* different now, Carly knew. The Saw's chomping path had changed the contours of it.

"We are in so much trouble," Carly commented as they ran. "We might never get out of here next time."

"I'm going to handle it," Gabriel said, trying to

hide the nervousness in his voice. He had to solve the tunnels. It was his job.

Luckily for now, the two left turns did the trick. They caught sight of the entrance to the Jackal compound. As they approached, the string of red lights flickered on.

"I think red means stop," Gabriel said. "Or proceed at your own risk."

Carly nodded. They'd missed that clue the first time. It wouldn't happen again.

This is way too dark," Ravi commented as the Omega crew ventured farther into the tunnel system. "Not cool. Not cool."

Suddenly a burst of red light lit the darkness ahead of them.

"We must be near the Jackal compound," Niko commented. "Those lights are not a natural phenomenon."

"We are in outer space," Siena reminded him. "We don't know what 'natural phenomena' we might encounter out here."

They crept closer. The gigantic bulbous lights did appear to be man-made. Creature-made. Handcrafted. Something. Niko wasn't sure what the right term would be for alien lighting installations.

"Colin says avoid the Jackals," Niko said.

"Do you see any Jackals?" Ravi countered.

"Avoiding them doesn't mean we can't take some advantage of their stuff."

They maneuvered through the corridor faster now that there was better light. They were working blind, otherwise. The map Colin had given them only showed how to access the tunnels from the planet surface. Inside, he'd told them, the tunnel layout was constantly changing. Even the Jackals hadn't figured out how to properly map the tunnels, though they were forever trying.

Niko spent a minute trying to take one of the lights from the wall. Siena hung by him, while Ravi wandered farther into the darkness.

"Yeah, this is not going to work," Niko determined. "They're all plugged in and attached."

"Not loving this planet so far," Siena said. "Let's all hope we have enough extra flashlight batteries to get back out."

"Hang on," Ravi said, reappearing suddenly from the black cave. "Forget about the light thing. I found something way better."

Gabriel and Carly returned to the hall of labs and resumed looking for Chris. Rather than retrace their steps, they headed in a different direction, following a string of yellow lights this time. The rooms in this section of the compound did not have glass walls. They were more like the study stations in a library, with carpeted half-height walls enclosing the different sections. The walls did not reach the ceiling, but were too tall to look over.

"Chris!" they shouted, but their voices only echoed off the compound's eerie walls.

They passed more and more cubicles, still deserted. They walked down either side of the hallway, poking their heads into each cubicle. Most contained a desk and some file cabinets. Very few had any more interesting items.

Carly prodded at her MTB, messaging Chris. "He's not answering."

"Maybe we're too deep," Gabriel suggested. It still wasn't working to contact the *Cloud Leopard* either.

"Or else he's too far away," Carly mused.

Gabriel found a neon-yellow-handled flashlight lying on a desk in one room. He brought it into the hall and flicked the switch a couple of times.

"It kinda looks like a black light," he said. "But it's broken."

"There was one of those in the lab with the safe," Carly said. "It didn't work either." Several more of the cubicles had them. None seemed to work.

Gabriel kept his anyway. It gave him something to do with his hands. He felt himself getting fidgety, itching to get on with the mission. He wasn't sure how much time had passed. It was probably still mid-morning, but between the dim lighting in the compound and the dark of the caves, it no longer felt like daytime.

"I'm getting worried," Carly said. "If we don't find Chris soon, we'll have to continue without him."

"It's weird that he just wandered off," Gabriel agreed. "Do you think he's okay?"

Carly shrugged. Who ever knew with Chris? This mission might be up to her and Gabriel alone. She had known it the minute Chris vanished—he was still keeping secrets. He had his own agenda, and Carly wasn't sure which priority would come first for him—the Voyager team's interests or his own mysterious intentions. Carly wanted to trust him—they had to! But it was hard when he was acting suspiciously.

At the end of the last row of cubicles was a large office. Carly's gaze zeroed in on a clear glass cabinet with stacked trays of syringes. They were all full, capped for individual use, and ready for injection. The glass doors had the slanted writing of the Jackal language etched on them.

"Ooh, interesting." Carly approached the cabinet and raised her MTB to access the translator.

Gabriel set the Jackal flashlight down on the desk. His hand brushed against the top. "Whoa." The bulb had grown warm to the touch. It didn't look like it was on, but something was clearly happening. An idea lit up in his mind—one that had been slowly heating along with that lightbulb.

"I wonder if . . . I'll be right back," Gabriel said.

"Where—" Carly started, but Gabriel was long gone into the hallway. She rolled her eyes.

Carly put the translator on to scan the words and translate them. She watched her wrist as the images scattered and turned from Jackal to English. Carly grinned excitedly as the translation came up.

Gabriel darted back into the room. "Hey, Carly, I have to show you what I found," he said.

"Whatever it is, this is better," she answered. "It's an anti-Stinger serum!"

"Excellent," Gabriel said. He rushed up beside her, and they opened the cabinet. "We'd better grab some of this for the road."

Carly reached in to extract a few vials of the serum.

"I'm not sure that's a good idea," said a voice behind them.

10

The voice sounded like a combination of a dog's bark and a cement mixer, low-pitched and grainy. Carly and Gabriel whirled around at the sound. A very tall, very thin, gray-skinned man stood in the lab doorway. Chris was beside him.

Carly glanced at the translator, already running on her armband, interpreting what the man had said. "I wouldn't try that if I were you," the gray man continued. "That serum has only been tested on Jackals."

Chris stepped forward, speaking the Jackal language fluently. "Carly and Gabriel, this is Colonel Ramos, of the Jackal Expedition and Research Contingent, also known as JERC." It was strange to hear the garbled words coming out of Chris's mouth and being picked up by the translator. "Colonel, these are the young humans I was telling you about. Carly Diamond and Gabriel Parker."

Colonel Ramos stared intensely at them. Carly

felt like they were under a microscope, as if the man's eyes could zoom in and out to capture every detail.

There was nothing to do but stand there and examine him in return. It seemed almost polite, under the circumstances. The man's features appeared to be a cross between a human and canine. Perhaps a rottweiler. He had those piercing eyes; a dark-tipped nose; long, sleek jowls; and a pointed chin. His hair was many shades of gray, streaked with black and white. His skin was gray and firm, not a wrinkle in sight.

"Take them away," Colonel Ramos told Chris. "I can't accept them."

"Accept us?" Gabriel echoed.

Colonel Ramos turned and spoke only to Chris. "They are truly intriguing, so you have me there. I'm happy to have given them a look, but it seems they would require significant care and feeding."

"Oh, no, sir," Chris hurried to explain. "You misunderstand. No care or feeding required."

"Really?" Colonel Ramos perked up. "Astonishing."

The colonel flared the tails of his jacket. He wore a suit made of Sawtooth leather, styled similar to a white-tie tuxedo. A "penguin coat," Gabriel recalled his father joking when they each had to wear one for his uncle's wedding. Colonel Ramos's lapels were decorated with what looked like Weaver feathers.

"Colonel Ramos is a busy man," Chris said, motioning the Voyagers toward the door. "We needn't bother him further."

Carly and Gabriel exchanged glances. What was Chris talking about? They needed the colonel's expertise for navigating the tunnels.

"Are you a military colonel?" Gabriel asked. He'd always thought it was a funny title for such a high-ranking officer—it always made him think of a kernel of corn. "Where's your army?"

Carly shot him a look that meant *hush up*. Gabriel shrugged. It was a reasonable question. The whole outpost seemed deserted.

"My colleagues have returned to our home planet."

"But you stayed?" Gabriel asked.

"I had nothing to go back to," Colonel Ramos said bitterly. "My work is here. My life is here. My purpose. The Jackal high command pulled our funding, ripped us all from our vital ongoing work."

"That's terrible," Carly said. "That happened on our planet too. Many rich countries pulled money from science research, even though our planet's in trouble. They sent us here to help solve the energy crisis. So we understand."

Maybe Colonel Ramos heard her; maybe he didn't. He stared through the empty glass cases, into the distance. "We had four dozen labs at our peak," he said. "Alone, I am able to maintain only six."

Carly wondered if the labs had once housed cutting-edge researchers. She could imagine the excitement and energy the place must once have held. It helped explain the feeling of sorrow radiating from the empty rooms, knowing they had once been vibrant hubs of activity.

"I'm sorry," she told him.

"It doesn't matter," the Jackal said, but even the electronic translation couldn't conceal the sorrow in his voice.

"So, you're really all alone here?" Carly couldn't imagine. It was hard enough being gone from Earth for a single year. The idea of never returning, ever, felt unbearable. "What about your family?"

Colonel Ramos glared at her. "Do not pity me. I chose this life." He stomped to a file cabinet and extracted a clipboard with a thick sheaf of papers attached to it.

He approached Gabriel. "Fine. I'll start with this one. Now, if you would, please." He indicated that Gabriel should stand with his arms up and imitate his own movements.

"What . . . ?" Gabriel wondered aloud as he followed the directions.

"This won't take long," Ramos assured him. "Range of motion, check. Language skills, check. General appearance . . ."

He circled Gabriel, examining him closely.

Finally he turned to Chris. "Does this race have a name?"

"I'm African American," Gabriel said.

"They are called human," Chris said. "From a planet called Earth."

"One male, one female?" Colonel Ramos made a notation on his clipboard. Then he brought out a tape measure. He took down Gabriel's height and the length of his arms and legs. He measured the circumference of Carly's head and the distance between her nose and chin, and the span of her palm from thumb to pinkie. When he reached for the other hand, he gasped.

Carly looked down. She had almost forgotten about the plant tendrils curled around her fingers.

"A mossflower." Colonel Ramos studied her closely. "Quite improbable."

"We found it in the tunnel," she told him. "Pretty cool, eh?"

"You do not find a mossflower," the colonel informed her sharply. "A mossflower finds you."

"I can't get it off," Carly said, nodding. "It's twisted itself onto me pretty tight."

Colonel Ramos looked at her for a long moment, as if he was trying to make a decision. Finally he spoke. "Some of my colleagues, the Jackal women . . . ," he began. Then he cleared his throat and shook his head.

"Just put it next to your face," he said gruffly. "Run your fingers through your hair."

Carly scooped the side curtain of her hair back over her ear. "Oh," she cried as the mossflower tendrils unwrapped from her fingers and twined themselves in her hair. The flower rested just above her ear.

"Best flower ever," Gabriel commented. "That looks awesome."

Carly smiled at Colonel Ramos. "Thanks."

With that, the colonel set the clipboard aside. "Chris, thank you for bringing them to me. They are indeed fascinating creatures. Much as I would love to examine them further, I'm afraid I am not taking on new specimens for study at this time."

Carly looked at Chris. "Specimens?" she said. "Didn't you tell him why we're here?"

"I'm afraid we hadn't gotten around to that," Chris said. He turned to Colonel Ramos. "Sorry for the misunderstanding."

"These are not gifts?" Colonel Ramos asked. "You come to my compound as a guest, with no hostess gift?"

"We brought gifts," Gabriel said. He reached into his pack and brought out the chocolate-chip cookies. "These are delicious. You're going to love them."

Carly got out the packages of hibiscus tea. "And

this. You just add boiling water, let it steep, and then drink it. Very refreshing." *Especially,* Carly thought, *if you're living all alone in a cool, damp place.*

"These are treats from their planet," Chris explained. "Treasured snack items."

"Very well," the colonel said. "Thank you. Put them on the table."

"You could experiment with how long to let the tea steep to produce the best taste," Carly suggested. "If you enjoy that kind of thing."

Colonel Ramos brightened a bit.

"And you could try to repeat the chocolate-chip cookie recipe," Gabriel said. "Cookie recipes are a big deal on our planet."

"Very well." The colonel made a few notations on his clipboard. "If that is all, be on your way, then." He bowed ever so slightly. To Chris, he said, "It was good to see an old friend passing through."

Carly stepped forward. "Colonel Ramos, actually we have some additional business on this planet. We hope you might be able to help us."

The colonel turned back to face her. "I'm afraid I can be of no help to anyone anymore," he said resignedly.

"But you don't even know what we need yet," Gabriel said.

The colonel sighed. "And what is that?"

Carly pressed on. "We're here to harvest Stinger spores."

Colonel Ramos laughed shortly. "Good luck. We lost many a scientist that way before we developed the serum."

"How'd you gather them?" Chris asked.

"We never determined a reliable strategy for retrieving Stingers without getting stung," Colonel Ramos said. "The risk is inherent, from the moment you enter a lake cavern."

"We have a plan, but we could use a few maps," Gabriel said confidently.

"And maybe borrow a few of your Weavers," Carly added.

The colonel stared at them for a long moment without moving or speaking. His dark eyes appeared unblinking.

"Can you help us?" Carly prompted.

"I will try," Colonel Ramos said. "If it will get you off my planet faster."

"Anyone ever tell you that you should chair a welcoming committee?" Gabriel said.

"No," said Colonel Ramos with sudden interest. "But I will make note of the fact that you observed this as an attribute." He pulled a worn spiral-bound notepad from his jacket pocket.

"I was kidding," Gabriel said, glancing helplessly at Carly, who was fighting back laughter. But

Colonel Ramos was already making furious notes, flipping page after page in the notepad. The spiral binding was sinewy, like Sawtooth skin.

Finally the colonel slapped the pad closed. "Come along, then," he said, striding toward the door. "Let's get this over with. The sooner you're dead or gone, the better."

11

"**Well, that's all** kinds of comforting," Gabriel said. Colonel Ramos had a thing or two to learn about hospitality. And tact.

"I guess we'd better follow him," Carly said as Colonel Ramos charged out of the room. She was still suppressing a grin.

Gabriel's expression was skeptical. "Are you sure that's a good idea? He seems a little . . . unstable."

"Be nice," Carly chided him. "He must be lonely."

"He is not lonely," said Chris. "He chose this life, several times over."

Even so, Carly thought, it must be strange and difficult to have been all by yourself for half a century. She had been away from her family for more than nine months now, and it was hard. How much harder would it be over fifty years?

If Colonel Ramos really didn't have a family, perhaps that was what made it easy for him to live as an explorer in another galaxy. But Carly thought there must be more to his story. She missed her own family tremendously. She even missed quibbling with her sisters over small silly things. The problems that sometimes came up at home seemed like nothing compared to the vast scope of the universe. Her love for them, on the other hand, stretched far enough to follow her all the way across the galaxies.

They followed Colonel Ramos through the compound. The kids had to hurry to keep up with the colonel's long, loping stride. He led them toward the Jackal's living quarters.

They passed briefly through a cozy denlike room. The stone walls had been painted a warm, homey brown, like dark wood paneling. Everything that wasn't upholstered in Sawtooth leather was furred with Weaver feathers. The room held couches in a U-shape and a tall armchair. Gorgeous carved-bone end tables and bookcases filled in the gaps. A black pelt of some sort spread across the floor. Gabriel had seen bear-skin and horse-hide rugs before; this Weaver rug followed along the same lines.

There was no time to look more closely at the Jackals' private habitat. They had to keep up with Colonel Ramos. Gabriel and Carly glanced at each other when they noticed the red lights blinking overhead. Colonel Ramos was leading them into the tunnels!

"Chris," Carly said hurriedly. "He's taking us out of the compound."

"I'm sure he knows where he's going," Chris said, but his voice was tinged with uncertainty.

They were in the tunnels only a few moments before they entered a spacious cavern. Low-wattage lights flickered on in a ring around the cavern at about waist height for Gabriel and Carly. Just enough light to see that the space was empty.

The large space must have originally been dug by Saws, but all the tooth ridges in the stone had been polished smooth. The gray cavern walls were so clean they shone. There was the tunnel they had come from, and two other exits. At least they had a way out if a Saw came a-slithering, Gabriel thought.

Colonel Ramos loosed a long low whistle.

Then there was a moment of silence, heavy with expectation.

A Weaver stallion rode out of one of the tunnels. His sleek coat glistened as he entered the lighted chambers, and the glow from his eyes dimmed. He tossed his mane and cantered toward them. He was the picture of elegance and pride.

"He's amazing," Carly whispered.

"This is Storm," Colonel Ramos said. "My own Weaver." He petted the stallion's neck. "I trained him from a colt. He's been with me many years."

The Weaver seemed wise and noble. He was clearly very old, with slivers of silver streaking his mane. When he heard his name, Storm pawed and nosed his companion.

Carly suddenly felt a bit better about Colonel Ramos's solitude. He had one friend in the universe after all.

"Hi, Storm," she said. She put out her hand, and Storm nuzzled it. His vapor breath dampened her palm. "You're beautiful," she told him. He breathed again, and she could feel the length of his life in that warm air. All the many years he had flown and fought and wandered.

"Why is he not penned with the others?" Gabriel asked.

"He is free to return to the tunnels," the colonel explained. "But he always comes back to me."

Carly was enamored by the large, gentle creature. Storm allowed her to rest her cheek on his muzzle. She patted his neck, letting the animal's comfort seep into her.

Chris watched her with his alien gaze. He seemed fascinated sometimes by human behavior and emotion. Carly too was fascinated by the idea of Chris's alien mind.

"You left us with the Weavers back there," she said to him. "What was that about?"

"I needed to find Colonel Ramos. There was something I wished to discuss with him. Privately."

"We're a team down here," Carly reminded him. "You shouldn't go off without telling us."

"I planned to return," Chris said.

Carly shook her head. "That's not the point." She took a few steps toward Chris. "We have to be able to count on each other. If we don't have trust, we don't have anything."

"I apologize?" Chris said, but he said it like a question.

Carly smiled gently. "Yes. You do."

"I shall consider your feelings and inform you before leaving again."

"Now you're catching on."

While Carly was talking to Chris, Gabriel pulled Colonel Ramos aside. "Sir, could I talk to you about the tunnel navigation system?"

"Indeed." Colonel Ramos stalked across the open room toward the tunnel Storm had come in through. As they got closer, Gabriel noticed that a patch of the wall was glittering. When Colonel Ramos reached out and touched it, ripples ran across the patch.

It lit up. Sort of like a computer screen, but made of some plasma-like substance. When the area grew bright, a giant digital map of the tunnels materialized.

Not a map, exactly. More like blueprints.

White lines on a gray-blue background. Green dots blinked from different layers of the screen.

There was no discernible pattern to any of it. Gabriel could barely tell what was supposed to be rock and what was tunnel.

It wasn't a clean rendering either. Some things had been scratched out, new ones labeled over them or beside them. The total effect made it look less like a computer screen and more like a new-age chalkboard.

"What are those moving dots?"

"Those Saws are tagged," Colonel Ramos explained.

"So you can track their movements?" Gabriel asked. He squinted at the map. The longer he looked, the more sense it made.

"Precisely. Of course, it is only a few."

The colonel swiped his slender fingers over the screen as if he was stirring soup. The plasma tugged and shifted under his touch. The map twisted. A genuine maze.

"There are many layers," Colonel Ramos commented. "Seventy-five thousand miles of tunnels and counting."

"Dang," Gabriel said. That distance would be

like going around the widest part of the Earth three times. Those Saws chomped like earthworms on some serious steroids.

Colonel Ramos swished and swirled the map.

"At present, this will be your best route to a lake cavern." A snaking golden line lit up, tracing a path toward the heart of the planet.

Gabriel quickly tried to memorize the route. He murmured to himself, "So that's a left turn, two rights, down a ramp taking us deeper . . ."

Chris came up behind them. "I do not suppose you have a portable version?" he inquired.

"No," said the colonel. "However, we do have this."

Colonel Ramos reached into his shirt and pulled out a pendant on a chain. He took it off his neck and handed it to Chris. It looked similar to dog tags.

"It will ping nearby Saws that are tagged."

"Brilliant." Chris placed the tracker chain around his own neck.

"The louder and faster the ping, the closer the Saw," the colonel warned. Chris nodded.

Chris's question about a portable map had given Gabriel an idea. He raised his arm and used his MTB to record the map. "This is great. Very helpful."

He didn't just take a photo of the map. He scanned it for several seconds.

"Remember, though, the tunnels will have almost certainly changed," Colonel Ramos warned.

Carly had an idea too. "Let me see that tag," she said. Chris held it out, and she studied it for a moment. It was just a simple receiver. Its only function would be to sense when the Saw tags were in vicinity, and how close. "Gabe, let me see your arm."

Gabriel held out his MTB arm and waited as Carly started tapping away at it. She used both hands, fast and furious, along the digital screen.

"Uh, what are you doing?" Gabriel said as she pecked away at him. It felt really odd to have some-one else working on his device.

Carly was hyperfocused. "Just . . . give me . . .

one second. . . . Yes!"

Gabriel's MTB pinged loudly. "Okay," Carly said, standing back. "I've written a program that should adapt the map as we go," she continued. "If Chris's pendant detects a Saw tag, it will show the movement on your map now."

"Awesome," Gabriel said. "Techie skills for the win."

"Well, you're the one who thinks you can lead us around the tunnels," Carly said. "The least I can do is give you the best possible shot." They grinned at each other.

Colonel Ramos observed these proceedings with detached interest. "There will be untagged Saws," he reminded them.

"We know," Carly confirmed. "We can only work with what we have."

Gabriel said to Chris, "You've got the Saw detector, so you should take the lead."

"You sure?"

"Yeah. I'll go in back and keep an eye on the map."

"Let's get going," Carly said.

"First, I'm going to take another scan of the map," Gabriel said. He pointed his MTB at the screen for a few seconds. "The faster we go now, the more accurate the map will still be."

They hurried through the hallways toward the stable. Strangely, the Weavers' corral seemed larger, and calmer, than it had a little while ago.

"Something's different," Gabriel said immediately. It slowly dawned on him what it was.

"Someone beat us to the punch," Carly said.

Three of the Weavers were gone.

12

The corridors of the *Light Blade* echoed eerily with the rest of the crew away. Anna stalked toward a narrow metal door near the engine room and flung it open. "How about in here?" she said. The small supply closet was just big enough for the two of them to step in and turn around.

Colin frowned, surveying the space thoughtfully. "Yes, that seems fine."

"The rest of the crew will never have to know," Anna added.

"I don't see why—" Colin began.

"You've lived on Earth," Anna snapped, cutting him off. "Surely you're familiar with the concept of an insurance policy."

"Indeed." Colin nodded. "I was going to say, I don't see why it needs to be kept from the crew."

Anna struggled to conceal the shadow of doubt that crossed her face. "They may not understand the need for such measures," she said. "It is not exactly playing fair."

ZRK PROBE DATA | PLANET INFINITY

LIGHT BLADE | PERSONNEL

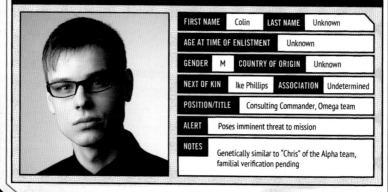

FIRST NAME	Colin	**LAST NAME**	Unknown
AGE AT TIME OF ENLISTMENT		Unknown	
GENDER	M	**COUNTRY OF ORIGIN**	Unknown
NEXT OF KIN	Ike Phillips	**ASSOCIATION**	Undetermined
POSITION/TITLE		Consulting Commander, Omega team	
ALERT		Poses imminent threat to mission	
NOTES		Genetically similar to "Chris" of the Alpha team, familial verification pending	

"It's a competition," Colin reminded her. "We do what it takes to win."

"We do what it takes," Anna echoed. The Alpha team had one major advantage over the Omegas right now. As soon as that threat was neutralized, the Omega team leader would be able to breathe easier. Dash Conroy acted gallant enough, but if push came to shove . . . well, he couldn't be trusted.

Anna eased back into the corridor with Colin and locked the closet door behind them. The most important thing was getting her crew home alive.

"It must be the Omega crew," Carly said, looking at the half-empty Weaver stable. The three remaining steeds gallop-flew faster and more swoopingly now that they had more space to maneuver. They looked incredibly majestic. Carly's fingers itched to hold the reins and ride.

"Dang it, the Omegas are going to beat us to the Stinger spores," Gabriel complained.

"There are plenty to go around," Chris said. "Trust me. That's not the problem."

"The problem is if you get stung," Colonel Ramos reminded them cheerfully. "If you do, try to get back here, so I can observe how the Stinger serum reacts in humans."

"Oh, sure," Gabriel said. "No problem. You can record each moment of our agonizing deaths in great detail."

"With pleasure," the Colonel agreed.

Carly laughed, but a chill went down her spine at the same time.

Colonel Ramos let loose three low whistles. The Weavers swooped down and lined up in front of him. They dipped and tossed their manes. They pawed their ghostly hooves.

The colonel brushed the mane of each steed with his long, slender fingers. "Thunder. Barrel. Knight."

Thunder was the one Carly favored. He was the tallest of the three. He had thick dark hair and his oval eyes glowed gently in the lamplight.

Gabriel moved toward Barrel. He was shorter and thicker through the middle. His stout legs shimmied as he stood in place, waiting. He nudged Gabriel's stomach with his nose.

That left Knight for Chris. The third horse seemed almost shy. He kept ducking his head and tilting away from the hands that reached out to stroke him.

Carly brought the saddles down one by one from the wall. They were as ethereally light as the Weavers' wings. Gabriel and Chris helped lash them in place over the Weavers' backs. They clipped on riding helmets. All three of them had to tighten the chin straps considerably. Jackals all must've had very long faces!

The horses stood still as the crew saddled up for the tunnels.

"Don't forget your swords," Colonel Ramos said. Chris brought over a pair of swords for each rider.

"Do we really need those?" Carly asked.

Colonel Ramos barked a laugh. He made no further comment.

Carly eyed the swords warily. The wicked blades intimidated her. Now that they had the maps, evading Saws should be the game plan. She looked at Gabriel. Surely he'd agree.

"Better safe than sorry," Gabriel said with a shrug.

Chris slid each of the six blades into the scabbards. They hung through, pointing down in front of the Weavers' wings.

The Weavers stood patiently as the riders climbed on. Carly and Gabriel had to reach above their heads to grasp the saddles and haul themselves up. Chris mounted smoothly, as if he'd been doing it for years. Carly wondered how long he'd spent here when he passed through the first time.

Colonel Ramos stood alongside and spouted riding advice. "Keep your knees tucked in. Gentle pressure on the reins."

"Here we go," Carly said, nudging Thunder toward the mouth of the tunnel. His eyes brightened as he trotted closer to the dark hall. Carly immediately knew the Weaver eyes would allow for much better visibility than her small flashlight had.

"Good luck," Colonel Ramos said. "Perhaps I'll see some of you again."

"Yup, it's official," Gabriel said. "You, sir, definitely have a future as a motivational speaker."

Chris and Carly laughed. Colonel Ramos, of course, made note of the observation.

"We'll see you," Chris said. "Count on it."

The three riders nudged their mounts, and the horselike creatures took flight.

"Whee!" Carly cried. Her Weaver's wings stirred the air. The breeze lifted her hair off her neck, and as she tugged the reins, the black horse dipped and tilted according to her whim. She could feel the creature's wildness, its spirit, but the Jackals had them impeccably trained. "This is amazing!"

Gabriel sat atop his horse, steady but uneasy. He clutched the reins with one hand and held the other loosely at his side. Chris held himself rigidly in the saddle, craning his neck left and right.

"Ready?" Carly asked, swooping ahead of the guys.

"Let's do it," Gabriel said.

They flew into the darkness.

The Weavers' glowing eyes lit the path ahead. Thunder's "headlight" beams washed over the scarred stone walls with the subtlety of oil-lamp light. It wasn't just like the effect of a stronger flashlight. The tunnels simply seemed to glow with light.

They rode three abreast for a short while, until the tunnel narrowed.

Gabriel nodded to Chris. "You lead us in. I'll lead us out."

"Go ahead," Carly said, reining in Thunder to allow Chris on Knight to go first, as they'd agreed.

Chris loosened the reins, and Knight charged ahead. Knight had the brightest eyes, and his shyness faded as he strained to get ahead of the others.

"The caverns have changed so much," Chris called. "It's nothing like I remember, and nothing like the map." His raised voice carried clearly, echoing off the stone walls. It was a bit like talking in a vortex, with sound being snatched and swirled and lifted by the Weavers' wind.

"Ramos warned us," Carly said. "The maps are out of date."

"And constantly changing," Gabriel said. His MTB lit up with the Saws' moving dots. Carly's adapted program seemed to be working. That, at least, was a good sign.

Some of the tunnels were as wide as a freeway, while others were as narrow as a country lane. Some vaulted high like church ceilings, while others were short and narrow.

I wouldn't want to meet the Saw that chewed its way up there, Gabriel thought as they flew through a high but narrow passageway. It was tall enough for the three Weavers to ride through stacked one above the other. Soon, the ceiling sloped back down and they were flying single file again.

Thunder instinctively avoided tunnels with Saws. Carly wasn't sure how he knew—if he heard or smelled or sensed the eels somehow. He would often snuffle or whinny an instant before Chris's tag pinged or Gabriel called out a course correction.

Which . . . hadn't happened recently, Carly realized.

Gabriel had been uncharacteristically quiet for a while now. Carly looked over her shoulder to make sure he was still behind her.

He was . . . sort of.

Gabriel was not flying straight. At all. The headlights on his Weaver zigged and zagged back and forth across the tunnel as he practically bounced off the walls.

"You okay back there?" Carly called.

"I'm good."

It didn't look like it to Carly.

"Maybe you're holding the reins too tight?" she suggested.

"I'm doing this on purpose," Gabriel called to her. "Don't worry about me."

I'll bet, Carly thought. But she didn't say anything else. Riding a horse wasn't exactly easy, she knew. Let alone a flying one. She didn't want to make Gabriel feel bad.

Gabriel continued his epic swooping, touching each wall as often as he could. It would be too hard to explain his plan in flight. Carly would understand soon enough.

Even though Chris was in the lead on Knight, Thunder seemed to be the senior Weaver. He whinnied and snuffled from time to time, and when he did so, Knight would instantly change course. The horses seemed to be communicating with each other on a level their riders couldn't understand. There was an order to things, in the Weaver world, apparently.

Thunder reared up suddenly, clearing his throat. They were approaching a Y, where the cave split yet again.

"Saws!" Gabriel called. "In both directions!" He could see the trajectory of two eels on his MTB. One was headed this way, coming straight down the right-hand tunnel toward them.

The left-hand tunnel looked clear for the moment. Gabriel studied his map again. The second Saw appeared to be in a side tunnel that would soon intersect with the main tunnel. And the image he was looking at could be several minutes old—there

was no way to tell how far the Saw had gotten since then. If they went left, they could fly directly into its path.

The lanyard on Chris's chest pinged softly. Then louder. And louder.

"Retreat!" Carly shouted.

"But there's a cavern just ahead," Chris answered. Down the left-hand tunnel, he could see the glistening lake.

"Can we get there before the Saw crosses?" Gabriel asked. On the map, it looked tight.

"We have to try," Chris decided. He nudged Knight to take the left turn.

Thunder followed reluctantly. He whinnied a warning as he flew. "I know, boy," Carly whispered. "We'll be careful."

It was worth the risk, possibly. The deeper they went into the tunnels, the more likely they were to get hopelessly lost. The water ahead glittered with promise.

But the tunnel was long. Longer than a football field, Gabriel figured. Halfway down, a second tunnel dead-ended into theirs. The Saw could be coming out of that hole at any moment.

Chris flew by the tunnel first. His lanyard emitted a loud, sustained pulse. He turned to look down the tunnel.

"It's close," he shouted. "Hurry!"

Thunder flapped harder than ever. He surged forward.

Carly didn't need to turn her head to look. The Saw arrived, just as she reached the intersection.

Snap.

13

"**What do you** mean it's working fine?" Dash bellowed. "Obviously it's not working fine, or we'd be talking to them!"

STEAM held up his robot hands imploringly. "I've run the diagnostics, yes sir. The ZRK Commanders have been in and out of the system as well. Everything is in order."

"Then why can we not reach them?" Dash lamented.

STEAM whirred and grunted. "Dozens of possible reasons, yes sir. Would you like them as a list, a graph, or a table?"

"Never mind," Dash said, tossing himself into his captain's chair. "I can imagine plenty of reasons all on my own."

"Imagination is a powerful thing, yes sir," STEAM said. "Like a runaway train, like a boulder rolling downhill, like a lion about to—"

Dash jumped up again. "How long do we wait

before we go down ourselves and try to figure out what's happened?"

"We can't," Piper said. The *Cloud Cat* was down at the surface. "We just have to be patient."

"What if they're in trouble?" Dash wondered aloud. "What if they need our help?"

Piper shook her head. "If there's some horrible trap waiting down there, we can't walk into it after them. The mission has to go on."

Dash really didn't like the sound of that. He knew Piper was just being reasonable and logical, but talk like that didn't do anything to take the edge off his worry.

Horrible trap.

The words echoed in his brain like clanging cymbals. A horrible trap, on Infinity.

Dash's eyes widened. Imagination was one thing. Memory was another. Dash remembered something suddenly, something Chris had said while they were in Gamma Speed.

"I've figured them out," Chris had said. *"The Jackals won't trick me again."*

They had been talking about the upcoming challenges of the new planet, just the two of them. Chris had seemed to think the dangers of this planet were more manageable than some of the others. *"Everything that might hurt you, you can see coming."*

"Let's pull up everything we can on the Jackals," Dash said to Piper. "There might be something we don't know. Something about them tricking people. Some kind of Jackal trap." Maybe Chris really hadn't told them everything he knew. Surprise, surprise.

"I was exaggerating," Piper said. She regretted the choice of words. "I don't think there's really a trap. I think they're just too deep underground." She tapped on her tablet screen, accessing the ship's database.

"What does it say about the Jackals?" Dash asked.

"It's a very short entry," Piper said. "There's even less than what Chris told us in the briefing."

"Read it anyway."

"'Jackals are hybrid humanoid-canine in appearance, bone structure, and musculature,'" Piper read aloud. She glanced up. "Do you want to see the picture again?"

Dash shook his head.

"'They are detail-oriented, highly intelligent, and strict in protocol. Their culture places a high premium on data collection and scientific research. Members of guest species are universally welcomed, afforded special quarters, and invited to extend their stay.'"

Dash waited for Piper to continue. When she didn't, he said, "That's it?"

"That's it," Piper reported. She paused. "What do you think that last part means?"

"Chris said the Jackals are big on hospitality."

Piper frowned. "What if it's not that simple?" Her brow furrowed thoughtfully.

"What are you thinking?" Dash asked.

Piper didn't want to say out loud what she was thinking. She was wondering about the nature of the "special quarters" and how firmly the Jackals' guests would be "invited" to stay.

"Nothing really," Piper said. "I was just wondering again if Chris actually told us everything we should know about the Jackals."

"'Invited to extend their stay,'" Dash murmured, already hovering around the same train of thought.

"I'm sure they're fine," Piper said, making her voice as upbeat and reassuring as possible. "It hasn't been that long, considering the tunnels and the Weavers and the whole scope of the mission. They'll check in as soon as they can. Until then, we wait."

Dash clenched his fists. Waiting, apparently, was not his strong suit. Doing something, anything, was better than doing nothing.

"Run the comms diagnostic again," Dash told STEAM.

"Repeat the procedure unnecessarily? Yes sir," said the robot, going to work on the console.

Snap. **The Saw's** jaws took off the corner of the rock wall. Carly and Thunder soared by in the nick of time.

Gabriel was about to be less fortunate.

He yanked on Barrel's reins. Luckily, his zigzag flight pattern had caused him to fall behind the others. Far enough behind that he had an extra few seconds to react. He narrowly avoided slamming smack into the Saw. Instead, he zigged ahead of it.

Barrel stretched his short front legs forward. He tucked up his back legs under his haunches as he vaulted past the snapping Saw. Its metallic jaws crunched down where Gabriel's body had been a split second before.

"Yaaah!" Gabriel cried as a cloud of the Saw's construction-dust breath overtook him. "Too close, guys. Too close."

"Are you okay?" Carly asked.

"I live for a wild ride," Gabriel choked out. He coughed and shook the cave crumbs off his shoulders.

Chris slowed to a stop. Knight flapped his wings and brought himself to a hover, then set down. Just up ahead, the tunnel gave way to a cavern.

Carly landed next to him. She glanced over her shoulder as Gabriel bounced off the wall a final time and stuttered to a landing. She wondered if he was too busy half crashing, or if he might be thinking

Chris tilted his head slightly. "You and I are not exactly 'men.' "

"It's a saying," Carly answered. "But I think you already know that." She dismounted, and strode ahead toward the mouth of the tunnel.

She found herself standing on the pebbled shores of a glistening blue lake. The Weavers' eyes illuminated the dim cavern beyond the threshold. Here, the walls were silvery smooth and slightly damp. They reflected the Weavers' light like mirrors.

Thunder reared back gently onto his hind legs and pointed his eye beams upward for a moment. The space stretched higher than his light could reach.

"It's gorgeous," Carly breathed. The scenery was postcard pretty. She stood for a while, appreciating the awesomeness of being one of only two Earthlings ever to set foot in the heart of Infinity.

"Extra cool," Gabriel agreed as he came up beside her. Carly noticed him shuffling with something along the edge of his belt. She couldn't see what it was.

The lakeshore sloped down from the tunnels to the water line. It consisted of glittering pebbles of all kinds of color. They glinted in the Weavers' sweeping eye-light. Some appeared solid and dark like rocks, while others gleamed with the transparent the same as she was—Chris's decision back a crossroads had been a little reckless. Racing a for no reason? They could have turned back looked for a safer route. The map showed plent other lake caverns in the area.

None of the rest of the crew would have ma that choice. Chris had endangered them, in favor what seemed easy. Did he care about them at all?

Carly tugged Thunder's reins until he walke up next to Chris on Knight. "You can't keep doing things like that," she said.

Chris looked at her. "What?"

"Putting us at risk without explanation. Acting like you're in charge."

Chris's eyes flashed with confusion. "The nature of the mission involves risk."

"Yes, but—" Carly began.

"I'm doing more to protect you than you realize," Chris said. "Everything has gone quite smoothly, in fact."

"We just almost got eaten. For the second time."

Chris appeared to be thinking. "Colonel Ramos has allowed us . . . Do you have any idea how many years it took me . . ."

Carly shook her head. He wasn't getting it. "On the ship, you can be mysterious and do your own thing," she told him. "On planet, we have to act as a team. It can't be every man for himself."

clarity of jewels. Carly was dazzled by the pebbled shore. She knelt and picked up one of the small stones.

"Sawtooth feces, I believe," Chris commented. "Undigestible impurities in the rock."

"Ewww." Carly wrinkled her nose and dropped the pebble. She rubbed her hand rapidly on her pants leg.

"Awesome!" Gabriel said. "The Saws poop jewelry?" He scooped a handful of the stones into his jacket pocket to take home with them.

Carly giggled. "Well, when you put it like that, it doesn't sound so bad."

A thick fuzz of moss grew on the walls, with clusters of gnats or flies buzzing around the largest moss clumps. Tucked within the moss patches, Carly noticed snaking green tendrils similar to those on her mossflower. But no more actual flowers in sight.

Finding the lake cavern was the first step to locating some Stingers. Carly looked up and could barely see the topmost reaches, even with the light of all the Weavers. Small things fluttered in the sky space above. Those must be the Stingers.

Behind her, Chris spoke softly. "Look where we are," he said. "You cannot imagine how long it took me to get this far, the first time. The Jackals keep a very close eye on their . . . guests."

Carly glanced back at him. On the ship, he had said he wanted to smooth things over with the Jackals for them. "What aren't you telling us?" she asked.

Chris stared into the lake cavern, like he was seeing some other place or time. "You don't need to know everything," he said. "You don't want to know everything."

Carly felt a flash of frustration. Who was Chris to decide what they needed or wanted to know?

"This place is huge," Gabriel observed. Looking up gave him a hint of vertigo. "How far underground *are* we?"

Two of the batlike creatures did a flyby. Gabriel flinched backward.

"They won't leave the cavern," Chris reminded them. "They need the moisture of the lake. The caves are too dry."

Carly watched as the Stingers zoomed for the moss clusters. Two tiny mouthfuls of gnats became Stinger food.

"Whoa." Gabriel stuck his hand across the threshold into the lake cavern. Amazingly, he could feel the difference. It wasn't like water on his skin or anything; it was more like stepping out of an air-conditioned building in the early summer. The air was instantly a few degrees warmer, and just a bit thicker. He sensed that if he went all the way in, he might begin to sweat.

The Weavers stamped impatiently along the lake cavern threshold, eager to cross inside and fly higher.

"It's okay, boy." Carly patted Thunder's mane. "You'll get your chance in a minute." The cavern was both inviting and a little scary. The tunnel felt like a protected space—you knew what was immediately behind and beside you. Once in the cavern, that certainty would be gone. The small flitting Stingers moved so fast it was hard to even see them individually.

"We'll need the nets ready," Chris said.

Gabriel had already unhooked his net from his backpack. Carly moved to free hers too.

At the far side of the cavern, a Saw slithered out of another tunnel. It wriggled across the sloping shore to drink from the lake. The slurping sound it made was almost as harsh as its chewing. The noise echoed in the cavern.

From above, a swirling cloud of Stingers descended upon the Saw. They landed on its back, their tails thwacking fiercely against its leathery skin.

"He's a goner," Gabriel lamented. He didn't feel particularly bad for the Saw. One enemy down, as far as he was concerned.

"The Saws are immune to the Stinger venom," Chris said. "In fact, I suspect the Jackals' Stinger cure serum is some distillation of Saw's blood."

"Are the Weavers immune?" Gabriel asked.

Chris cocked his head. "I don't know," he said. "The Jackals never seemed worried about it. I'm sure they've studied the question."

That did not sound promising. Carly stroked Thunder's muzzle. She didn't want anything to happen to him. Would he be risking his life to help them?

"The Stingers won't fly too close to the Weavers anyway," Chris said. "That's why we need these long poles."

"Let's go get 'em," Gabriel said, climbing astride Barrel again.

The Weavers pranced restlessly once all the riders were on board. They were eager to enter the cavern.

Carly figured it must be okay, if they were so excited.

They rode into the cavern. Chris circled low, aiming for the bunch of Stingers crowded around the thirsty Saw. Barrel took Gabriel through some sinewy swirling loops above the water. Thunder apparently could not resist flying highest. Wind whipped through Carly's hair as he carried her up, and up some more.

It was beautiful. She could have simply soared with him forever, but she had to keep her mind on task.

Carly nudged Thunder toward a collection of Stingers parked on craggy stalactites near the ceiling.

They hung like bats, talons clutching the uneven surface of the rocks.

They looked like easy pickings. But as Carly drew close, the Stingers' slack wings began to ruffle with the wind from Thunder's much larger wings. The Stingers stirred and took off, fleeing the area. Carly and Thunder gave chase, but the swift little creatures got a good head start.

Below, Gabriel and Chris were having a similar problem. Fly close enough to reach, and the Stingers would flee. The same thing happened, over and over.

The problem soon became obvious. The Weavers' wings did keep the Stingers at bay—too much so. The Stingers were not flying close enough to catch with the nets. The net poles were not long enough.

"We're making wind, so let's use it in our favor," Gabriel suggested.

The three flew to opposite sides of the cavern. Then they flew toward each other, and the Stingers got pushed together by the wind. They swirled into a mass in the center.

Gabriel, Carly, and Chris leaned forward, extending their poles. They dragged their nets through the Stingers, in a scooping motion.

Carly frowned in frustration. Even working together, not very many Stingers had gotten into her bag. She tried to swipe again, but the batlike creatures escaped upward, toward the craggy recesses of the cave.

She closed her net's drawstring to keep the few she had gotten. Very few. It was not looking good.

After ten minutes of trying, Gabriel and Carly landed near the tunnel again. They trotted into the safety zone and stopped to compare notes. They sat side by side astride their Weavers and studied the glittering lake.

"This isn't working," Carly said.

Gabriel nodded. "I know."

There were seven Stingers in Carly's net, about ten in Gabriel's, and only four in Chris's. He landed beside them and showed his tiny haul.

"These Weavers are larger than the ones I based my calculations on," Chris admitted. He glared, almost angrily, at the net pole he'd created. "It's not long enough. I should have realized this could happen."

"It's going to take forever to get enough," Carly said. "We need hundreds more."

Gabriel stared into the cavern. Only one solution came to mind. "I hate to say it, but—"

"—we need to go in on foot," Carly finished.

"Yeah."

"Except—"

"—it will probably kill us."

"Yeah."

"Just a tiny little glitch there."

"Very tiny."

"I'll stay with the Weavers," Chris said, helpfully.

Carly and Gabriel glanced at him. Was he serious? They couldn't really just walk into the chamber. They didn't actually want to die. Chris took things too literally sometimes.

"Yeah . . . That's not actually going to work," Carly told him.

"How long are their stinger barbs, again?" Gabriel asked.

"Half an inch," Chris answered.

"I have an idea." Gabriel dug into his pack and unzipped the pouch containing his Simu Suit. When it sprang free, he fingered the foam, feeling its thickness.

About two inches.

"That might do," he mumbled.

Gabriel slid off of Barrel, who snuffled nervously and tucked in his wings. The other two Weavers also folded their wings and stood perfectly still, in deference to the human now on the ground among them.

"What are you doing?" Carly demanded.

"Trust me," Gabriel said, zipping himself into the suit. "I've got this." His body was fully covered now, except for his fingers and face. He felt behind him to secure the place where his riding helmet met the back of the Simu Suit, protecting his neck. Then he tucked the ends of his sleeves into his fists and drew his fingers inside.

Carly's eyes widened as she realized what he was planning to do. "Are you crazy?"

"Just crazy enough." Gabriel grinned. "Wish me luck," he called as he plunged headlong into the cavern.

14

Dash stared at the *Cloud Leopard*'s communication console, wondering if he should run another diagnostic on the equipment. Things had been quiet for way too long. "Come on. Doesn't it seem weird that they haven't checked in even once yet?" he asked aloud. "At least to say 'all's good' before they went underground?"

Piper hovered in her air chair nearby. "Mm-hmm," she answered, distracted.

"Weird, unusual, out of the ordinary? Yes sir!" STEAM piped up from the other side of the room.

Dash glanced at the small robot, who was ever eager to please. "Thanks, buddy," he said. "But I was talking to Piper."

"Hmm?" Piper said again.

She had been studying her tablet intently for over an hour. Her free hand idly stroked the top of Rocket's head. He sat alongside her chair, his chin resting on her knee.

"How can you just sit there and read?" Dash blurted out. He resumed his restless pacing, glaring at Piper.

Piper looked up from her tablet. "I'm worried about them too," she said softly. "Reading helps keep my mind off it."

Maybe Piper was right. He needed a distraction too. "What are you reading?" Dash asked, trying to remain calm. Conversation might help keep his mind from drifting.

"I'm doing some research on the Stinger spores," she said. "They are pretty intensely bad. But really fascinating."

"It talks about them in your medical journals?"

Piper shook her head. "Chris gave me a report written by the Jackals. They've spent decades examining the spores inside and out. Chemical breakdowns, physical properties, potency of the primary toxin."

"Wow." Dash was happy Piper was the ship's medic, not him. It didn't sound like his idea of pleasure reading, but she was grinning enthusiastically.

"Their research methodology is extremely meticulous," Piper said. "They leave no stone unturned, you know?"

Dash wasn't sure he knew, but he nodded. He had a sudden flashback to fifth-grade science class and his experiment on batteries. He had just had a conversation with Carly about how awesome but weird it was to be missing a whole year of school during this mission. Everyone on the crew felt like they were still learning a lot, even though they hadn't set foot in a classroom in months.

"Are you going to start running more experiments yourself?" Dash asked with trepidation. Piper seemed to enjoy the activities in the science textbooks they had on board.

"Oh, yeah," Piper said, excited. "As soon as we leave Infinity."

There was always plenty of time while they were in Gamma speed for her to study. She grinned at the good-natured skepticism on Dash's face. "I just read some articles about blood typing. It sounds really fun. Will you mind if I draw some blood from you? I mean, more than usual, for the med checks? There's a kit down in my—"

The communications console lit up suddenly. "*Cloud Leopard,* this is the *Light Blade.*" The landscape on the display screen disappeared, and Colin appeared, looking haggard.

Or, at least, as haggard as an emotionless evil alien clone can look.

Rocket barked twice. It sounded like a warning.

Piper moved closer to Dash as he turned to face the screen. It was always a bit startling to see Chris's face reproduced on Colin. The glasses made a difference, but not quite enough to stop the double take.

"Dash, we've got an emergency." Colin's cheeks looked slightly flushed. His breath came out in panting jerks. "It's Anna—I don't know what to do. The ladder just slipped, and—"

"Whoa, wait." Dash held up his hands to stop Colin's breathless tirade. "What happened?"

Colin took a deep breath. "Anna has fallen from a great height," he said, resuming his normal, almost robotic tone. "She does not move, does not answer."

"Oh no," Dash said. His pulse sped up. An accident in space—he had been fearing this for his own crew. If Anna was seriously hurt, what would it mean for the mission?

Piper zoomed forward in her air chair. "Is she breathing?"

"I do not know," Colin said. "But I fear she is significantly injured."

"Is she bleeding?" Dash asked. "How far was the fall?"

"She hit her head on the way down," Colin said. He paused. "I'll go get her body and bring it here so you can see."

Body? Dash thought. That sounded terrible.

"No! Don't move her," Piper told Colin. "Moving her could hurt her more."

"What should I do? Can you help, please?" Colin begged. He looked shocked, motionless.

"I'll go," Piper said. "I'm the medic."

Rocket barked two more times.

"Shh," Piper soothed him. "It's okay, boy."

"The *Cloud Cat* is down on Infinity," Dash said. "We couldn't go even if we wanted to."

"I don't need a landing craft to fly, remember?" Piper zipped toward the cargo door. "I'll get my medical kit."

"We're still in orbit," Dash reminded her. "You'll need booster rockets on your chair."

"And a space suit, I know," Piper called over her shoulder. "I'll meet you in the engine room."

Dash knew Piper was right. Helping out the Omega crew was the right thing to do. So why couldn't he shake this bad feeling?

He zipped through the tubes to the engine room. Rocket bounded in from the corridor and barked twice, nudging Dash's knee. STEAM waddled in moments later and found Dash studying the collection of rockets, various spare parts for the *Cloud Cat* and the other smaller crafts.

"What about a couple of these?" he asked STEAM, pointing to a set of four rocket canisters for the landing craft. Each was the size and shape of a toddler's Wiffle bat.

"Will they burn long enough to get her to the other ship?"

STEAM's database whirred, calculating speed,

distance, trajectory, atmospheric density, the weight of Piper in her chair. "All four together will do the trick, yes sir," he reported.

Piper floated in, wearing a space suit. The round plastic helmet rested in her lap, atop her medical kit.

"Are you sure about this?" Dash asked.

"Of course," Piper said, clipping her helmet into place.

Dash lashed the booster rockets by their necks to the sides of Piper's air chair, while STEAM attached an oxygen canister to the back and connected it to her helmet hose. Since her head was now sealed inside the bubble, Piper gave a thumbs-up.

Dash drew back into the safety of the ship, leaving Piper alone to launch from the engine room. He watched on the screen from the flight deck as she punched the door release and the cargo door eased open. The rockets fired, and Piper's air chair carried her into the white sky. The door closed behind her.

For a while, she was a large dot on the console screen, then a small dot, then she faded from view.

Rocket darted in a close circle around Dash's legs, before parking himself on Dash's right foot. He looked up with large, sad eyes, the tip of his tongue out. Dash let his fingers glide through the golden retriever's fur. Rocket seemed worried too.

"What are the odds she makes it back all right?" Dash wondered aloud.

Across the flight console, STEAM 6000 began beeping and whirring. "Incalculable," the little robot answered. "Too many variables unknown, yes sir."

"She'll be fine," Dash assured him. "Piper can take care of herself. It was a rhetorical question."

"Hmm," said STEAM. "Very well, then."

Miles below, down in the depths of Infinity, Gabriel sumo-stomped his way into the lake cavern. The beefy Simu Suit made it hard to move quickly.

"Come and get me," he shouted.

He didn't need to say anything. The Stingers instantly responded to the motion of the intruding creature. They dove at him in swarms.

Gabriel held his padded arms up like a shield over his face. He waddled forward down the embankment until he heard his boots splash in the water.

Through the Simu Suit, he felt the Stinger wing beats slapping lightly against him. Everywhere. Some of them were getting downright personal.

"Yaaah, they are getting all up in my grill!" Gabriel fought the instinct to slap them away. He had to keep his face covered. Luckily, he wasn't feeling anything sharp.

"This is crazy," Chris muttered from the edge of the tunnel.

"Crazy brilliant," Carly amended. "Come on, let's help him out."

She nudged Thunder into flight. Chris and Knight followed. They swooped through the cavern from opposite directions, using the Weavers' wind to drive more and more Stingers toward Gabriel.

Carly looked down from above and found that she could barely see Gabriel. The thick cloud of Stingers engulfed him.

Gabriel was noticing the same issue himself. An issue that was quickly becoming a full-fledged problem!

The Stingers thumped and jostled him.

Gabriel struggled to stay on his feet. His arms and legs were suddenly heavy. Too heavy to move. Too heavy to stay upright.

He fell to his knees. Water soaked into his Simu Suit, weighing him down further.

His arms, so heavy now, dragged him forward. Toward the water. He had no choice but to let his head and shoulders follow them. Otherwise, his face would be exposed. He'd be stung to death in seconds.

No! He could drown!

Almost too late, he realized the danger he was in. He twisted his body to the right. It took all his effort. He landed on his elbows in the pebbly muck. The lake lapped against his cheek. He gasped for breath in the wake of each wave.

Stingers still pounded him from above. Relentlessly.

They were making sounds, he realized. Amid the lull of the lake and the voices of his friends above, he could hear them.

The Stingers emitted a low melody, barely audible. Like singing. It was eerie, and soft, like catching a hint of music floating from a very distant room.

It was a lovely sound. More lovely by the moment. He could relax now, he thought, and just listen. . . .

"Gabriel!" Carly's shout from above drowned out the tiny, pleasant voices.

His mind snapped back into focus.

Stingers . . . not singers!

They would kill him eventually.

Probably sooner than "eventually."

Terror sliced through him. He tried to move, but he couldn't. There was too much weight upon him.

He had made a huge mistake.

Carly and Chris soared overhead. Carly craned her neck. Gabriel's form had gotten smaller, it seemed. She flew closer and saw him crumpled in the shallow water.

"He's trapped!" Carly cried.

The weight of the Simu Suit, plus the Stinger pellets, plus the pull of extra gravity on Infinity . . . Gabriel was completely stuck in place!

"We have to pull him out," Carly shouted. His arms, in the padding, were still covering his exposed face, but who knew how long he had before a Stinger barb found its way between the cracks.

Chris wheeled Knight around. "I'll stave them off," he called. "You help Gabriel." With that, he nudged the Weaver's haunches and swooped downward. The wind stirred the Stinger cloud. The bat-like beings spiraled upward.

Carly landed and dismounted. She raced on foot into the chamber.

The Stingers swirled toward her en masse, but Chris rode through ahead of her and Knight's wing blasts drove them back. It seemed like he was finally starting to grasp the concept of teamwork.

Carly grabbed Gabriel by the shoulders of his Simu Suit. Her fingers squeezed into the foam and water ran out. The suit felt knobbly, studded with Stinger pellets.

She hoped that they couldn't poison her through her skin. The spores had to be injected to cause damage, right?

She had no choice. The Stinger cloud shifted, poised to return.

Carly dug her fists into the Simu Suit.

"Up on three," she shouted. "One . . . two . . . three!" She hauled Gabriel to his feet.

Gabriel put all his effort into standing upright, but the lopsided weight of the Simu Suit dragged him back down. He flopped onto his stomach.

"Oh, no you don't," Carly yelled. "Come on."

Gabriel's feet skidded against the moss. There was no way he could stand.

Carly clutched his padded shoulders and tugged. She backed her way steadily out of the chamber, dragging him along.

Chris circled above and kept the nearby air free of Stingers.

"Okay, now stop squirming," Carly grunted at Gabriel. "I think you're making it worse."

She used all her strength to drag him inch by inch along the slick mossy pebbles of the lake shore. "Didn't . . . exactly . . . think . . . this . . . plan . . . all . . . the . . . way . . . through . . . eh?" She eked out one word per breath as she tugged him up the embankment.

"It seemed like a good idea at the time," Gabriel muttered. His voice was muffled by the edge of the Simu Suit.

"Clear!" Carly shouted to Chris as she successfully drew Gabriel across the threshold of the tunnel. She unzipped his waterlogged suit and helped him climb out.

When he was free, Carly clapped Gabriel on the back. "Always knew you were nuts," she commented.

"Crazy is the new awesome." He did a funky little dance. "Can't touch this."

"Touched . . . in the head," Carly muttered, grinning good-naturedly.

Chris landed his Weaver on the bank and dismounted.

Gabriel helped Carly pull the Simu Suit farther into the tunnel. It was heavy, even without him inside. The Stinger pellets must've each weighed a ton.

"How do they fly with these things in their butts?" Gabriel wondered.

Carly laughed. "Do you think we got enough?" she asked, turning serious.

"Sure feels like it. And I can't believe you had to drag me out of there," Gabriel said, slightly chagrined.

Carly smiled again. "It'll be our secret."

"No chance," Gabriel answered. "That was way too awesome. I'm telling everyone!"

They laughed together, as they plucked Stinger pellets from the suit with tweezers and pliers from Carly's toolkit. They plopped them one by one into the jar, counting carefully as they worked. Hopefully Gabriel's crazy trick meant they had gathered enough—but it was much better to find out now than back on the ship.

The Weavers, who had been standing at perfect attention, suddenly whinnied and shuffled their hooves. Thunder looked over his shoulder, shining his eyes into the tunnel.

Chris stood up and darted into the tunnel. "We gotta go," he said when he returned a moment later. His chest tag pinged.

"But the spores," Gabriel said. They were still tweezing and counting. They hadn't even finished the arms.

"We're only at two hundred fifty," Carly said.

There was no way to refold the suit all the way with the spores inside.

"Squeeze the water out, and get it on the horse," Chris said. "We've got a Saw coming."

15

Piper floated across the Infinity sky. It felt infinite, for sure. No clouds. No wind. Only the light hum of her chair, and a breathtaking view of the pure blue sky and the craggy gray surface below. Oxygen hissed into the dome of her helmet, and she breathed calmly, gazing through the plastic shield. She was worried about Anna, but she couldn't help appreciating the scenery. It was an amazing feeling to be flying in the open air, on another planet, across the universe from home.

Piper had never felt like her wheelchair was holding her back, but it did make her different from her friends. There were times when she missed the feeling of running or jumping. It was special and cool to be able to do something no one else could. She stretched her arms out against the sky as she flew. The heat from the blazing booster rockets below warmed the sleeves of her space suit.

The *Light Blade*'s cargo bay doors opened to allow

her entry. Colin stood on the *Clipper* launch pad, an expression of grave concern on his pale face.

He looked exactly like Chris, except for the glasses. Piper did a double take upon seeing him in person for the first time. It was really uncanny. Even weirder than seeing a large-scale statue of him—which, oddly enough, she had also done.

"Hi, Colin," she said. "Where's Anna?"

"Right this way," he said, gesturing formally for her to proceed alongside him into the hallway.

Piper took in her surroundings. In some ways, the *Light Blade* seemed similar to the *Cloud Leopard*, but it was more . . . sinister. The ship had been shadowing them for months, and it felt like a shadow in here. It had an unfinished quality to it, exposed pipes and wires running along the length of the hallway. And it was dim. Piper half expected things to start leaping out of the walls at her, like in a haunted house. A back-of-the-spine, tingling sensation crept over her.

"You are the medic, correct?" Colin said.

"Yes. What's happened, exactly?" Piper asked, hovering along next to him. He moved a bit too slowly, she thought, for someone in the middle of a crisis. She chalked it up to his cold, alien nature.

"Anna has fallen from a great height," Colin repeated. "I fear an injury of the skull or spine." He stopped walking then and began fumbling with something he pulled from his pocket and held low at his side. Piper tried to turn to see what he was doing, but being side by side with Colin, the hallway space was narrow for that kind of maneuver.

Five seconds later, Piper screamed at the top of her lungs.

At that very moment, two miles below, Siena screamed at the top of her lungs. A cloud of Stingers swooped toward her. The flock shifted as if of one mind, with one goal: to devour her. It was an amazing sight . . . and deadly.

Siena slashed her net pole through the flock, then dove for the edge of the lake cavern, stumbling across the pebbled shore and flopping to safety on the cold cave rock.

The winged cloud surged upward, skating along the cavern wall. They dispersed above. They swirled the air like a tornado.

"We can't . . . keep . . . doing this . . . ," Siena panted, pulling herself up onto her hands and knees.

"How many do we have?" Ravi asked.

"She got two more," Niko said, checking Siena's pouch. Exposed to the drier tunnel air, the Stingers lay limp inside the netting. "That's ten total. At this rate, it's going to take hours."

"Days," Ravi amended.

"And possibly kill us all," Siena added, trying to keep her voice cheerful. She wasn't sure why, when the situation was clearly so bleak. She gazed down the dark tunnel. Not dark. Pitch-black. "They're really not coming back, are they?" she said of the Weavers.

"Obviously not," Ravi snapped.

When the Omegas ran into the chamber for the first time, the horselike creatures had galloped away into the tunnels. It had been a mistake to let go of their reins, apparently. A lesson learned the hard way.

"I was just saying," Siena muttered. She was not looking forward to leaving the cavern behind and returning to the dark caves on foot.

The flashlights from their packs barely made a dent in the wall of night. Ravi's flashlight, set to the lantern mode, rested on the stones just inside the cavern. That and a stream of light from a crack in the rocks high overhead were all that saved the cavern from total darkness. The pale light reflected off the water, giving the cavern the ambience of a moonlit summer lake.

"We can take these few back with us to the ship," Ravi suggested. "They're not like bees—one sting. They'll make more spores."

"I don't know," Siena said. "Bringing home live Stingers wasn't part of the plan."

"So we change the plan," Ravi insisted. He waved his hand toward the lake. "You wanna go back in there?"

"We have to keep trying." Niko agreed with Siena. They had to carry through the plan. He picked up his pole. He was next to plunge in.

As if sensing Niko's intentions, the Stinger cloud reformed. The winged things hovered, waiting to descend.

"Great," Siena said.

"How about no." Ravi stared into the dimly lit cavern. "We've done all we can do. Let's get out of here."

From the flight deck of the *Cloud Leopard*, Dash reopened the comm link to the *Light Blade*. The screen showed the flight console, empty.

"Colin?" Dash called, hoping he was just off-screen. "Colin, is everything all right over there?"

Long tense moments passed.

"Hello? Colin?" Dash tried again.

The screen flickered to a different angle. Piper's face filled the screen. "Dash!" she cried.

Dash's pulse pounded at the alarm in her voice. But he was relieved to see she had made it over there okay. "How's Anna? What happened?"

Piper shook her head. "You were right!" she said. "It was—"

The screen flipped again. Dash found himself staring at Anna's grinning face.

"Why, hello, Dash Conroy. I knew we could count on you."

"Are you okay?" Dash asked. Anna looked none the worse for wear.

Anna laughed. "I have never been better," she said. "And Piper will be fine too. Eventually."

The camera panned out. Behind Anna, Piper floated helplessly on the bridge of the *Light Blade*, struggling to free herself from the ropes binding her to her air chair. They stretched across her chest, pinning her in place, and her wrists were tied behind her. Her legs hung free, as motionless as ever.

The truth hit Dash hard. Anna was never injured. It was a trap! And he'd fallen for it, hook, line, and sinker.

"Let her go," Dash demanded. He jumped out of his chair, as if to run and help her. But there was no way for him to get from one ship to the other without the *Cloud Cat*.

"I could do that," Anna admitted. "But this way, you'll be sure not to lose us in Gamma Speed."

"You already have Pollen Slither," Piper said angrily. "You don't need a hostage." She wished they would lock her in a room or tie her to a post. She hated having her air chair used against her. Even more, she hated that she'd let her guard down, thinking the Omega crew really needed her help. It had been far too easy for Colin to lasso her wrists with the rope. Something like this never would have happened during a mission. She should have been ready for anything, even here. "Let me go!" she shouted.

"We're not going to ditch the *Light Blade* in space," Dash insisted. "We would never do that."

"A little extra insurance never hurt," Anna said.

"You won't keep her," Dash said. "You can't. We'll never leave this planet without her."

"We'll see about that," Anna said. "The mission comes first."

"No, my crew comes first," Dash insisted.

The words spilled out before he even had time to think. He meant them, from the bottom of his heart.

And yet . . .

Eighty-four days remaining in the mission, with two planets still to visit. If Anna and Colin wanted to play hardball in a standoff over Piper, could Dash afford to wait them out?

16

"Hurry," Chris urged. The Saw slithered and gnawed its way closer.

Carly and Gabriel used their weight to press on the Simu Suit's foamy limbs. Water poured out of it in seemingly endless streams. Their hands began to ache from pressing against the hard, knobbly pellets within. There was no way the suit would fold up as small as usual with all that baggage inside it.

Chris was monitoring the Saw's approach. "We can't get ahead of it now," he said finally. "The side tunnel is no longer an option."

Carly looked up in alarm. "It's past the nearest crossroads?"

"It's probably coming here to drink," Chris said. "We'll have to wait inside the cavern."

They folded the Simu Suit as best they could and hefted it up behind Carly's saddle. They secured it to Thunder's haunches with rope that they lashed to the saddle straps. Thunder had the longest body of the three Weavers, and he didn't seem to mind terribly having a mess of damp foam strapped to his rump. He calmly allowed them to work on him, as if he understood the importance of his duty.

They climbed onto their Weavers. Barrel trotted willingly toward the water.

"Great," Gabriel grumbled. "Back into the lion's den."

"Aww," Carly said, nudging Thunder forward. "But the Stingers just *love* you."

Gabriel shot her a withering glare as they soared up into the cavern. They waited, protecting themselves from Stinger assault with the Weavers' beating wings.

Below, the Saw slithered its toolshed-sized face into the water.

"Tunnel's clear. Let's get out of here," Carly said.

"You got me out of the cavern; I'll get you out of the tunnels," Gabriel promised. He and Barrel took the lead. "Let's just hope that Saw didn't completely mess with my plan."

"You have a plan?" Carly asked.

"This is my coup de grace," Gabriel assured her. "My biggest trick ever. Check it out." He pulled one of the Jackals' special neon-yellow-handled flashlights from his backpack and powered it on.

In the darkness, the light that had been too pale

to see earlier shone like a lantern. Like Weaver eyes, almost. Except the light cast a slightly darker, stronger beam. Carly could see it pointing ahead even though the tunnel was aglow with Weaver light.

Gabriel swung the beam upward, and it reflected off a patch of something high on the wall.

"Is that paint?" Carly asked.

Gabriel nodded.

"The paint from the safe?"

"Yup. It *is* a tunnel navigation system," he said, laughing. "It's just a super low-tech one." He flourished the light like an orchestra conductor waves a baton.

Carly laughed too. "I guess so. Lead us back, maestro!"

She and Chris followed as Gabriel led the way through the tunnels.

"So this is why you've been bouncing off the walls?" Carly called.

Gabriel grinned. "Go ahead. Doubt my methods. I won't mind. I'll be too busy saving our lives."

"And to think, I was feeling bad for you, not being able to fly straight," Carly said. She was relieved to know Gabriel wasn't such an inept rider after all. There was a method to his madness. "This paint trail's gonna get us out of here?"

"You better believe it."

The beat of the Weavers' wings made a soft

shushing noise around them. When the shushing grew louder, they almost didn't notice until it was too late.

"Saw!" Gabriel shouted. He yanked on the reins and Barrel reared back. Carly's and Chris's mounts reared back in echo, before they even had time to react.

A Sawtooth Land Eel, moving much faster than the ones they'd encountered earlier, shimmied toward them through the tunnel. The gnashing teeth sounded like construction equipment.

"Quick," Gabriel screamed. "Get back, get back!"

The three Weavers, acting on instinct no doubt, whinnied and wheeled around. They swooped away from the oncoming Saw, plunging back into the dark. It was a minute before Gabriel realized he was no longer actually steering his ride—the Weaver was flying in whatever direction it wanted. He quickly tightened the reins, and Barrel slowed to hover in place while the others caught up.

Gabriel shone his light on the walls nearby. No sign of paint. "Uh-oh."

"Lost the trail?" Carly said.

"We have to go back, then," Chris said.

"Straight into the jaws of death?" Carly said. "I don't think so. What's plan B?"

"Uh . . . we could try to loop around." Gabriel consulted the map. "This way."

He unsnapped the paint can at his waist. "I'll start marking the trail again, so at least we can get back to this place later, if we need to."

Gabriel drew a giant G on the wall.

Carly grinned. "Leaving your mark?"

"You better believe it." Gabriel raised the brush triumphantly, the way track runners do after crossing the finish line in first place. "I was here."

The Saw snapping behind them drew closer. Gabriel kept his brush at the ready as the Weavers bolted through the tunnel to stay ahead of the giant jaws.

They circled to the right. It should have been a full circle, like going around the block. It should have led them back to their old trail, but it didn't. Gabriel saw no sign of his previous marks.

And it felt like they were going down, deeper into the planet, not up toward the surface, Gabriel thought. They had to get back. He led them onto the next upward facing turn, and—

"Oh no."

They were back at Gabriel's giant G. He reined in Barrel and hovered as he stared, horrified, at his own handiwork.

"And you wondered why they call this place Infinity," Chris said dryly.

"I've lost the trail completely," Gabriel admitted. "We took a really bad turn somewhere." A hopeless, sinking feeling descended upon him. Navigation was his responsibility. He had let the team down. They might be lost in these tunnels forever.

"I think we only took one turn the first time," Chris said. He pointed. "Back there." The Saw that had originally chased them to this point would be long gone by now. They could double back the way they came.

"Maybe we can find the trail again," Carly said. "We have to keep trying."

"Okay," Gabriel said, more confidently than he felt. He led them back, shining the dark light over the walls. Nothing.

Nothing.

Nothing.

Finally . . .

"Aha!"

Gabriel paused as the light glanced over the smallest snippet of a paint blotch. It had to be his own, from earlier. The genius of the Jackals' special paint was that its potency faded over a matter of hours, Colonel Ramos had told him. Within a day or so, the trail would be gone forever—so as not to lead future travelers in the tunnels astray.

Gabriel had his bearings now, but the area was still not safe. The sound of snapping jaws echoed from the tunnel ahead. They couldn't see the Saw yet, but one was definitely coming. And untagged—Gabriel's map showed the whole area around them as clear.

"That's the way we need to go," Gabriel said, pointing in the direction of the sound. He'd lost the trail once. It wasn't going to happen again.

"Uh, we can't . . . ," Chris said. "Start marking. We'll just have to retrace our steps again later." He started to retreat down the tunnel, but wheeled around almost immediately.

"If we stand here, we definitely die," Carly reminded him. "That Saw isn't stopping for pleasantries."

"Neither is that one," Chris said, pointing in the opposite direction. A second Saw!

They were cornered.

"Not again," Gabriel cried. The desperate sinking feeling of impending death washed over him, for the third time today.

Three strikes, you're out, he thought. He couldn't stop his mind from screaming it.

He'd gotten lucky that his Simu Suit plan hadn't sunk—literally.

They'd gotten lucky in the dead-end tunnel earlier too. But he couldn't imagine a secret crevice big enough for three people, plus three Weavers and a messed-up Simu Suit.

Carly pulled on Thunder's reins, turning him about. "What now?"

Chris reached down to his saddle sideboard. He drew the long sword. "Now we fight."

17

Dash stood between STEAM and Rocket on the flight deck, staring at the empty sky through the view screen. None of them had moved in quite a while.

Dash's mind raced, contemplating possible rescue scenarios. The war was raging on two fronts now—Piper trapped on the *Light Blade,* and Carly and Gabriel still underground. At least they had Chris down there with them.

Piper was completely alone.

But Dash had no way to get to her. Even STEAM's robot brain had been unable to come up with any mechanism that would allow him to fly across the chasm of space without the *Cloud Cat* or an air chair.

Every inch of his body burned to *do* something. But there was nothing he could do.

Dash turned to Rocket. "What about you, boy?" he asked. "You got any ideas?"

Rocket barked twice and sat, curling his tail around his feet. He gazed up at Dash with sad eyes.

"Okay, fine," Dash said, struggling to tamp down the fire in his gut. "We wait."

The two Saws closed in on the Alpha crew members from opposite directions.

"What happens when they meet?" Carly asked. This twisted scenario hadn't exactly come up in the mission brief.

"We can't let that happen," Chris said, drawing his sword.

"Surely they don't eat each other," Gabriel said.

"They'll battle for supremacy, then one of them will turn," Chris said. "Or else the fight will cause this tunnel to collapse."

Gabriel didn't even want to think about that option. He swallowed hard. "One will turn . . . and make a new tunnel?"

Chris nodded. "We don't want to be in the middle of that."

Carly felt a tugging sensation behind her ear.

The mossflower!

Perhaps, once again, the strange plant was trying to help. The stem tendrils curled around her hair drew themselves upward in three swift jerks. Then three more.

Carly looked up. Her gaze scanned the surface

of the stone. There was nothing but ceiling. No strange cubby or chimney to tuck into. Nothing miraculous.

"What?" she whispered, hoping the flower could hear.

The tendrils tugged upward again. The petals flapped against her ear, like wings.

Wings . . . Could it be?

Carly nudged Thunder forward. The Saw behind them filled almost the entire tunnel, but the oncoming Saw was smaller. The tunnel ahead was high, and growing higher.

"This tunnel might be tall enough," Carly suggested. "We can fly over him!"

"I am not sure . . . ," Chris began. His sword was drawn and ready to fight.

But Carly felt more and more certain. This was what they had to do.

"Thunder, can we do it, boy?"

The Weaver whinnied and stirred his wings. He soared toward the ceiling. He stretched his back legs back and his front legs forward, as if he was landing a competition fence jump.

Carly bent close over his neck. The Saw's chewing crunch grew loud and close. Carly closed her eyes, leaving the work to the Weaver. His firm muscles under her gave her confidence. He could make it work. Maybe he'd done it hundreds of times before.

Gabriel and Chris swooped through the narrow gap after her.

"Tight squeeze!" Gabriel commented once they were clear.

"Not as tight as getting gnawed," Chris said, sounding matter-of-fact.

"Like threading a needle," Carly added. "Equine style." She patted Thunder's neck.

They rode on, Gabriel marking the tunnel walls as they went. Soon a snarling sound echoed behind them. The Saw fight!

Gabriel looked over his shoulder. "I wonder which one will win."

"The larger one, naturally," Chris said. It seemed quite obvious who had the advantage.

"My money's on the little guy. He seemed scrappy," Carly said.

"At least that was the worst that can happen," Chris said.

Gabriel cringed. "Never say things like that, man!"

Chris shrugged. "It's logic. The scenario we just encountered was of the worst type we could encounter."

Gabriel groaned again. "Stop it now. You'll jinx us."

Chris, of course, did not subscribe to human

superstition. "I made no claim that we won't find ourselves between two Saws again."

"Yeah, well. That's what hope is for."

They came to another crossroads. "Which way now?" Carly asked.

"Right," Gabriel said.

"You always choose right, and we always end up in trouble," Carly commented.

"I always choose right, and we're still alive," Gabriel amended.

Carly couldn't argue with that.

They turned right.

"It feels like we are going deeper," Carly called after a while. "Do you think that's best?"

Gabriel slowed Barrel. The Weavers landed and circled up so their riders could speak.

"Let's look for an alternate exit," Chris suggested. "There may be something closer. And we would do well to avoid a return to the Jackal compound."

"Why?" Gabriel asked.

"We can avoid a difficult negotiation," Chris said.

"No," Carly demanded. "We need to know what is going on."

Gabriel agreed. "We're not moving until we know the truth."

A dozen yards down the corridor, a horrible crunching sound rose. A Saw burst through the wall, moving perpendicular to the existing tunnel. It slithered across the opening, gnawing at air, then continued. A helpful reminder: they couldn't linger long.

"Tell us," Gabriel insisted.

Chris sighed. "The Jackals are scientists, as well as . . . collectors."

"Collectors?" Carly echoed "Of what?"

"Specimens. Species. Anything they can get their hands on to study."

Gabriel nodded. "So . . . this is why he thought we were a gift. He wants to add us to his collection?"

"For scientific study?" Carly was aghast.

"Probably not Colonel Ramos," Chris reassured them. "Not anymore. We got lucky that he's the only one left."

Gabriel was steamed. "How could you not tell us? You let us walk straight into a trap!"

"A seeming trap," Chris acknowledged. "I've outsmarted them once. I could've done it again. Much faster."

"Why not the colonel?" Carly asked.

"He saved my life back then," Chris said. "He considers us friends."

Gabriel snorted. "With friends like these, who needs enemies?"

Chris shot him a cold look. "With Colonel Ramos's help, I evaded the Jackal clutches once. But it took more time than you can fathom."

"How exactly did you escape?"

Knight shuffled his feet and whinnied. Chris held his reins fast. "That might be a story best told when we are safely back on the *Cloud Leopard.*"

"Let's find the way out," Gabriel agreed.

Less than a minute later, the dark tunnels ahead lit with the pinprick glow of oncoming lights.

"Wild Weavers?" Gabriel wondered. But the lights were too small to be Weaver headlights.

"Not wild, and not Weavers," Chris said. "It's the competition."

He saw the others before Gabriel and Carly did. But they only had a moment to be puzzled before they understood.

Ravi, Siena, and Niko came racing out of the darkness, carrying flashlights.

"Saw behind us!" Ravi shouted. "Get out of the way!"

The Saw was coming up fast and furious. Faster than any they'd seen yet. The Omegas were running full-speed to stay ahead of it.

"Ride with us," Carly offered. She landed Thunder, and Siena leapt on board behind her.

"Thanks!" Siena shouted. "Ew, why is it all wet?" She glanced over her shoulder at the sodden mound of Simu Suit strapped to Thunder's haunches.

"Don't have to ride if you don't want to," Carly muttered. Siena stayed put.

Ravi joined Gabriel on Barrel. Niko hopped on

behind Chris as the Saw came chomping closer with each passing heartbeat.

They pushed on through the tunnels, back the way they had come. The Weavers made quick work of leaving the Saw in their dust.

So much for the alternate exit. They found themselves following Gabriel's paint trail again.

"What happened to your Weavers?" Carly asked.

"We lost them in the caves," Siena said. "We had to park them to catch the Stingers, and then a Saw came. We couldn't get back in time. They got spooked and flew off."

That was when Carly noticed that Siena held a writhing mesh bag in her hand. Full of Stingers!

"Yikes," Carly said. "Are those things secure?"

"Sure," Siena said. "Their tails can't fit through the mesh."

"There's another cavern ahead," Gabriel shouted. He could see it on the map. "Go right!"

They emerged into a vaulted atrium about half the size of the lake cavern.

It instantly became clear that Chris had been wrong earlier. There was definitely something worse than being caught between two approaching Saws.

Siena screamed.

Carly screamed. She twisted Thunder's reins in an effort to turn back, but the guys and their Weavers were right behind her. They'd been flying fast, one after the other. All she could do was dive down and to the left to avoid crashing into a jutting spire of rock.

Siena yelped and dropped her bag of Stingers. She held tight to Carly as Thunder dipped and dodged through a sudden minefield of thick protruding rocks that stuck up from the ground and hung from the ceiling. Stalactites and stalagmites big enough to carve statues of horse and rider.

Behind them, the guys also panicked. They flew whatever direction they could.

"Yaaah!" Gabriel shrieked.

Something that sounded like "You've gotta be kidding" choked its way out of Ravi.

This cavern wasn't full of open air. It was nothing but a mess of small tunnels and carved-out nestles in the rock. Tunnels too small for the Weavers to fly through, and most of which were already occupied anyway.

Because this cavern also wasn't even really a cavern. It was a den.

18

They were stuck in a room with dozens of Saws. Saws in the walls, on the ground, in the doorways.

Carly counted six full-grown Saws at first glance, plus a mess of smaller ones. Tiny tunnels wove in and out everywhere. The littlest Saws wriggled like worms around the cavern.

Little might not have been the best word. They were small for Saws, but still huge compared to the humans in their midst. The smallest ones were four or five feet tall—about the same height as Carly.

Saws slithering. Saws chewing. Saws drinking, from a small lake nested at one side of the cavern. They lay on the pebbles and slurped lazily while a small contingent of Stingers assaulted them from above. It looked like they were doing whatever the underground Saw equivalent of sunning themselves might be.

The new generation of Saws had chewed out a small network of caves in the rock. Big enough for a human to enter, perhaps, but not a Weaver. The cavern that had looked spacious on the map was much more of an obstacle course in real life.

"No!" Chris exclaimed. He jerked Knight's reins upward. Niko wasn't expecting the sudden movement. He lost his grip and slid right off the Weaver's back, landing smack in the middle of a circle of small Saws.

Niko shook off the pain of the fall and dragged himself to his feet. He found himself face to face with the young Saws. They were learning to work their jaws through trial and error. They gnashed them in no particular direction.

He spun in a circle, looking for a way out. He was surrounded.

The youngest Saws' cries sounded like an infant rattle, like several dozen throats gargling stones they hadn't yet learned how to swallow.

He had nothing with which to fend them off.

Chris swooped overhead on Knight. The circle of Saws was too small for the Weaver to land.

Chris drew the sword from his sideboard and stabbed at a little Saw's snapping jaw. It ground its teeth in agony and flailed closer to one of its brothers, allowing space in the circle. Niko darted through, headed for the smaller tunnels.

"Stab them," Chris called to the others. "They'll be confused. But they'll also regenerate. And fast!"

"We have to help Niko!" Carly cried. She landed Thunder at the edge of the cavern and dismounted. She hesitated only a moment before she pulled the long sword from the saddle sheath. Siena grabbed hold of the opposite one.

"Let's try to clear him a path from the tunnel to the door," Carly said. "But . . ."

"We'll have to work together," Siena agreed. The two girls met each other's eyes. In a life-or-death situation, the competition between their ships shouldn't matter.

"Here goes nothing." Carly held the sword tightly and ran back into the den.

It was much too hard to fly around in the den. Too many rocky obstacles. Gabriel and Chris landed their Weavers too.

Niko had run all the way back through the small tunnels toward the lake. He was running in the wrong direction, but who could blame him? He was preoccupied by goal number one: do not get eaten.

It was up to the others to help him find his way out. And it was going to take a hefty dose of teamwork.

Niko reached the edge of the cavern's small lake before he realized he needed to turn around. Stingers flitted by, and he dove for safety in a drier part of the cavern.

The others worked their way across the room, dodging and slicing through baby Saws to get to Niko. They all tried to help make a path out for him, but they got cornered by a massive Saw.

Before long, the Voyagers stood back to back, fighting in a circle. They dodged and parried, moving wherever they could to stay alive. Chris ran bravely to and fro among the Saws swirling, slicing and then trying to roll them away.

The large Saw was about to become the real problem. It slithered right toward the ailing smaller ones, looming over Chris. The Saw was fifteen feet tall, with a maw the size of an average living room. They could've all sat down to dinner in its mouth, Gabriel thought, and he laughed out loud at the sudden image. The crazy kind of laugh. The "we're all about to die" kind of laugh.

The Saw's tail extended easily eighty feet, and it was partly coiled, to boot. It was thick and long, sealing off the exit with its bulk.

None of their swords were long enough to even hope to strike its head. All they could do was jab and prick, and it only seemed to make the Saw grow angry. They teased it in tandem from all sides.

Stab, dodge.

Stab, dodge. Finally the rhythm started to move her away from the tunnel. The small ones wriggled away toward safety, as if responding to some warning.

Now the Voyagers had the largest Saw surrounded.

Suddenly, Ravi realized that he, Siena, and Niko were all on the tunnel side of the mother Saw.

The Omegas could get out. Safely.

Ravi grabbed Siena's arm and tugged her toward the tunnels. "Run!" he shouted to Niko. "We gotta get out of here."

Niko took in the situation. His head was spinning from the rapid pace of battle. He'd gotten a few good swipes in on that massive Saw's tail, but Ravi was right. It was time to go.

Niko stumbled dizzily toward the exit. His head was slightly pounding from all the exertion.

"But—the Alpha team," Siena cried as her crewmates urged her back into the tunnels. It was wrong to leave them behind in such peril.

"Forget them," Ravi said. "We're safe. That's all that matters."

The three Omega team members raced into the tunnels on foot. It was not ideal compared to riding the Weavers. And there were Weavers right there for the taking.

"Come on," Ravi said, grabbing Barrel's reins. "Let's use these."

"No way," Siena said. "How will the Alphas get back? We have to wait for them."

"We were fine on foot and they will be too," Niko said. He hopped onto Knight.

Siena turned toward the third Weaver. It gazed patiently back at her.

"Get on with me, if you want," Niko said. "The faster we get out of here the better."

Siena turned back toward the mouth of the Saw den. Guilt stole over her. Carly and Gabriel were surrounded.

"Hey." Ravi held up two bags of Stingers—his and Siena's. "I've got the goods, if that's what you're worried about." He had seen her bag on the ground and picked them up during the Saw fight.

"Come on, or we'll have to leave you too," Ravi urged.

Moment of truth. Siena could run back into the Saw den and help the Alphas.

And possibly die.

Or, what if, in the end, they wouldn't let her join them?

Siena ran up alongside Niko's mount, which was Knight. She vaulted herself into the saddle behind him. "No reason to leave them totally stranded," she said. Guilt and shame strapped her heart. It was so, so wrong to leave their friends behind like this. *Enemies, not friends,* Siena tried to remind herself. But the idea wouldn't quite sink in.

The Omega crew flew off into the darkness. The

metallic gnashing of Saw teeth faded into the background.

Back in the Saw den, the gnashing remained a very urgent problem for the Alpha team. Alone now, with no one to distract the large Saw from the other side, it closed in on them. Chris stumbled toward its tail, hoping to find a narrow spot to slice. Maybe he could get her to turn all the way around. But her coils made her tail thick. His sword strikes didn't seem to be affecting her at all.

Carly and Gabriel ran from the huge snapping jaws. They staggered toward the smaller tunnels, breathless. But they couldn't go too far too fast; a mess of small Saws waited right up ahead.

Worse—as if it needed to get worse—a flock of Stingers swirled down at them.

"We're too close to the water," Gabriel observed. He could feel the slickness of moisture on his skin.

"What do you suggest we do about it?" Carly cried. The small Saws were in front of them, gnashing innocently around for something to sink their teeth into.

"Get back to the dry part of the cavern!"

"Easier said than done," Carly grumbled, brandishing her sword. She turned around, ready to face the larger Saw again.

Carly slid on the pebbles. She fell onto her

back with a thump that knocked her breath away. The sword clattered to the ground beside her. She stretched, but it was just out of reach. A small Saw slithered right on top of it, grinding it down into the bed of jewels.

Carly jerked her hand back.

The large Saw nudged the young one out of the way and closed in on them.

The Saw's teeth snapped with the usual amount of menace. Close up, it was like looking into the mouth of a garbage crushing machine. Rows of teeth, going back as far as Carly could see.

Beside her, Gabriel instinctively curled away from the biting jaws. Stingers were close now. No foam suit to protect him this time. The death sting would come at any second.

Carly and Gabriel looked at each other, one last desperate glance.

It was over.

All was lost.

"Aieeeechwagrrle!" The harsh chortling sound of dogs in a cement mixer echoed through the cavern. The air stirred with the fresh beat of Weaver wings. The flock of Stingers spiraled upward, retreating toward the highest reaches of the cavern. The Saws slithered away toward the water, sensing a danger they could not see.

The largest Saw hissed in agony as it was

stabbed by swift, deep blade strikes from above. It reared its head and then flopped to the side.

Carly and Gabriel scrambled toward safety as Colonel Ramos, brandishing one long silver sword in each hand, swooped through the chamber on the back of the eldest Weaver, Storm.

19

Colonel Ramos and Storm took command of the chamber in short order. When Carly lifted her head from the glittering gravel, the Stingers were nowhere to be seen.

Colonel Ramos was shouting. He whisked his sword through the air and pierced a second large Saw through the forehead. The two large Saws writhed in agony. One plunged herself into the water, startling the small ones. The other crashed against a wall of mini tunnels, bringing down their walls. It coiled on the rubble, nursing its wounds.

They were not dead, Carly reminded herself. Only temporarily disabled. Not that she'd mind the colonel killing those nasty things.

Colonel Ramos waved urgently at the kids, gargling at the top of his lungs.

Gabriel twisted on the ground, reaching to tap his MTB to translate.

"He's saying to run," Chris said. "Get out of

here while the Saws are disoriented. He'll hold them off."

The Alpha crew scrambled up to the mouth of the tunnel. They raced to the spot where they'd parked the Weavers. Thunder waited quietly, alone.

It took a second before it dawned on them what must have happened.

"No way," Carly said. "Those jerks!"

"Left us behind AND took our ride?" Gabriel huffed. "Figures."

"I can't believe it," Carly murmured. For a while there, it had felt good, working together with the Omega crew. It was how it should've been all along, Carly thought. And then they went and did something like this. Her chest ached with anger as she tried to catch her breath. "At least they left us our spores."

"I bet they wouldn't have," Gabriel said bitterly, "if they'd realized what it was."

"What do we do?" Carly wondered aloud.

"We'll just all have to get on this one," Gabriel said. "He should be able to carry all of us."

Carly boarded Thunder, and Gabriel climbed on behind her. He scooted as close to her as he could, to leave room for Chris. But there wasn't enough space—not with the Simu Suit strapped on Thunder's haunches.

Chris told them, "No, you go ahead."

Carly turned Thunder's tail toward Chris. "We can fit."

But Chris backed away. "I don't want to leave the colonel," he said.

"We're safe now," Carly said. "I'm sure he'll be right behind us."

Chris turned back, toward the cavern. The rest of the mother Saws were gathering. The split ones were regaining their strength too. The colonel and Storm fought nobly, but they were surrounded.

Then, all of a sudden, the elder Weaver wasn't flying anymore. He landed in the middle of the chamber, and folded his wings. Astride his back, the colonel sat steady, swords in hand as the Saws closed in on him.

Carly felt a sudden jolt of terror. "Colonel! Come with us. Come now!"

But the path to the door was already blocked by a refreshed mother Saw. The colonel closed his eyes and raised his swords.

"Colonel Ramos!" Gabriel yelled.

"I'll help him," Chris said. He had the only remaining sword of the three. He ran on foot toward the chamber.

Gabriel nodded. "We're coming with you."

Chris called over his shoulder, "No. Return to the ship. For you, the mission must come first. Always."

Carly and Gabriel exchanged a glance. No man gets left behind. The mission was to bring the elements back to Earth, but they needed to be able to do it with their heads held high. The Omega crew might be out for themselves, but the Alpha team was all for one.

Without a word, Carly wheeled Thunder around and swooped after Chris, back toward the Sawtooth den.

20

The communications console on the *Light Blade* lit up suddenly. Anna jumped up from her chair. Ravi's voice filled the speakers. "Hey. We're almost done. Heading back to the ship now."

"Excellent," Anna said. "Everything go okay?"

"Well as can be expected," Ravi reported. "Considering a brief run-in with the Alphas. Pretty sure they're still stuck down there."

Anna grinned. Her crew would be back first, Stingers and spores in hand. *Take that, Alphas,* she thought. She ended the call with Ravi and opened up a call with the *Cloud Leopard*.

"What is it?" Dash snapped. "Ready to send Piper home?"

"My team is on their way back," Anna informed him. "We'll be ready for the Gamma jump soon. I'm just letting you know."

"We won't jump without Piper. Not in a million years," Dash insisted, his angry face filling the screen. "We'll live on Infinity. We'll die on Infinity. And so will you."

Anna laughed. "Never take up poker, Conroy. You're no good at bluffing."

She punched the button to end the call.

Now the monitor screen showed Piper, tied in the storage room belowdecks. Anna clicked it off entirely. The rest of the Omegas might have to know Piper was with them eventually, but for the moment, she'd keep the information to herself.

Chris ran into the Sawtooth den, dodging the small Saws. He ran straight toward Colonel Ramos, unstoppable. Chris shouted something to the colonel, who answered, "No, leave me!" over and over. Chris grabbed the reins and started leading Storm out of the chamber.

Thunder swiftly carried Carly and Gabriel across the cavern threshold, then flew in very tight circles overhead.

"Who's got the crazy now?" Gabriel commented, watching Chris slice his way back toward the exit.

"We can't stay in here," Carly said, suddenly alarmed. "We have nothing to fight with." Without swords, it would be insane to dismount. And there was really no place to fly. Thunder hovered in a holding pattern, softly whinnying in frustration.

Gabriel surveyed the scene from above, with a

navigator's eye. "Chris needs a path to the exit. We can't do much, but we can keep the doorway clear."

Carly nudged Thunder downward. He used his hooves to pound the head of a mother Saw, confusing her until she went inert.

"Now, Chris!" Gabriel called while Carly was busy at the reins.

Chris boarded Storm behind the colonel. The elder Weaver stirred, as if waking to the fact that his work was not yet done. He unfurled his wings and carried both aliens through the cavern exit.

Carly and Gabriel's Weavers swooped down after Storm, escaping the den.

"What are you doing?" Colonel Ramos shouted. "Why? Why?"

"Gabriel, take the lead," Chris called over the colonel's wailing laments.

Gabriel examined his MTB for Saw activity. He could take charge. He *should* take charge. He was the navigator after all. He knew he had left a good trail this time, and the special flashlight was at the ready. In fact, Carly was already nudging Thunder into the lead position, ready to follow Gabriel's commands.

Gabriel fought down the sudden hunger that arose inside him. This was his moment. Dash wasn't here to be the boss of him. He could lead the crew out of Infinity, and everyone would be grateful.

He could already feel what a thrill it would be to take credit for saving the day. In the *Cloud Cat*, he never hesitated to switch off autopilot because he knew he could do it as well—or better—on his own.

But sometimes, teamwork meant *not* taking charge. Not hogging the glory unnecessarily.

"We should follow Storm," Gabriel decided, clicking the flashlight off. "Colonel Ramos says he always finds his way home."

It was the right choice.

Given free rein, Storm and Thunder, with their Weaver sixth sense, swooped through the tunnels as if they could clearly see the way ahead. The pair of Weavers found the Jackal compound without any further confusion or delays. Coming home, it seemed, came quite naturally to the creatures.

They swept into Storm's private cavern and landed gracefully, shaking out their wings.

Colonel Ramos dismounted in a huff. "You mad humans!" he screamed. "I gave you a way out. I gave you victory!"

"We all survived, Colonel," Carly said.

"That's the real victory." Gabriel was confused by Ramos's anger.

"Fools!" The colonel stalked furiously toward his chambers. Carly and Gabriel rushed to follow.

Chris untied the Simu Suit from Thunder's haunches and freed the Weaver of his saddle. The

Simu Suit had dried somewhat, but it was still a heavy mess. Chris dragged it into the Jackal residence.

He caught up with the others in time to see Colonel Ramos throw himself into his tall armchair.

The colonel hung his head. "Why did you return for me?" he lamented. His jowls shook.

"We couldn't leave you to die," Gabriel said.

"Of course you could! The warrior's way out is always painful."

"You're a scientist first," Carly said. "What about your experiments? What about returning to your planet one day?"

Colonel Ramos blotted his forehead with his sleeve. "Small humans. You do not listen. I shall never return."

"You don't know that. What if you change your mind?"

The colonel regarded them coldly. "There is much you do not understand about the universe."

Carly supposed that was true. "I'll make you a cup of tea," she offered. "That might help you feel better." She retrieved a bag of hibiscus tea from their gift box, which was resting on the coffee table. Chris pointed her toward a spigot in the food preparation area. Gabriel tore into one package of chocolate-chip cookies and gave two to the colonel. "Try this too."

The colonel grudgingly accepted the offerings.

He stuck his long gray tongue into the teacup, then sniffed the edges of a cookie. He scowled deeply over his first bite, and downed the boiling beverage in a single gulp. Then he sniffed the cookie again.

"If you really don't want to go home, you could come with us," Carly said.

Gabriel nodded. "Yeah, come with us. We could use a great scientist like you back on Earth."

"Small humans," the colonel repeated before the remainder of the cookie disappeared into his mouth.

Carly and Gabriel glanced at each other. It was a good idea, they thought. The colonel wouldn't have to return to his planet, but he also wouldn't have to be alone.

"You should have left me in the Saw den. It would have been the best way to go out," Colonel Ramos said quietly. "In a blaze of glory, defending the innocent. It would have been a worthy end to a life like mine."

There was silence in the room for a moment. The silence of abandoned labs, of empty caves and tunnels. The silence of long, long lonely years.

"We're sorry," Gabriel said finally. "We didn't know."

"You're saving us a great deal of sadness," Carly told him. She laid a hand on the Jackal's shoulder.

"It would have been awful for us to leave knowing you had sacrificed yourself."

Gabriel agreed. "Or worse, wondering for the rest of our lives whether you had survived," he added. "So really, you're doing us a favor. By, you know, still being alive."

Colonel Ramos listened intently to their words. Ultimately he turned to Chris. "This human race," he observed. "They are full of feelings."

Chris smiled. "It is one of their defining features."

"Very well," the colonel said. "Leave me be for a time. I will be done in a minute." With that, he turned toward the wall and sunk himself deeper in the chair, loudly lamenting still being alive.

Carly and Gabriel sat on the carpet, painstakingly tweezing out the spores. They plunked them into the jar one by one as Chris counted them. When they were done, Ramos had fallen quiet.

"The total is nine hundred and ninety." Chris reported the number in a matter-of-fact tone.

Carly hung her head.

Gabriel slapped himself in the forehead. "Noooooo. So close and yet so far."

It would be awful to return to the *Cloud Leopard* with fewer than a thousand spores. They needed the full thousand, or the whole mission had been pointless. But the very thought of going back into those tunnels, back to the lake cavern . . .

Wait!

Carly perked up. "Hang on, what happened to that jar of spores we found in the lab? There were more than twenty in there."

"But they were old," Chris reminded her.

Gabriel dug into his backpack. "I've got them right here." He shook the jar. You could hear the difference the age made—their dry husky sound versus the full, damp, meaty feeling of the fresh spores.

Colonel Ramos gradually removed the arm that was draped over his eyes. He stuck out his hand. "Here. Let me see them." He straightened up and examined the jar of dried spores.

"They are not so old, really," he determined. "I can measure their potency, if you like."

Ramos brought out some strange-looking tools—the apparatus vaguely resembled a miniature oil rig. He measured the potency of the old spores. "Roughly fifty percent," he reported. "So, fifty micro-units of the Stinger toxin. Per spore."

Carly quickly did the math. "It's enough!" she cried. The dried spores were going to save them. "We did it!"

She bounded toward the colonel and hugged him tight. "And your measurements let us know for sure. We couldn't have done it without you."

He patted her back awkwardly. "Well, I suppose I am good for something every century or two."

"See," she said, slugging his arm good-naturedly. "You've still got game."

The corner of the colonel's mouth twitched upward. "I do not know what this means, to have 'got game.'"

"Yeah, you do," Gabriel said. He grinned, delighted to see the colonel finally fighting off a smile.

"Won't you come with us, Colonel?" Carly offered again.

"We have plenty of room on the ship," Gabriel reminded him.

"This is my home," Colonel Ramos said, returning to his usual stiffness. "And the life I have chosen."

"Please?"

"Leave me be," Colonel Ramos said. His expression had barely changed, overall, but Carly believed he was gazing at them more fondly. "There are many experiments still to be done. For instance, next I shall try to master the chocolate-chip cookie."

21

Tears slipped out of Carly's eyes as the three made their way up to the *Cloud Cat*. She'd tried everything she could think of, but nothing seemed to matter. Colonel Ramos refused to leave with them.

"I couldn't leave my debt unpaid," Chris had whispered as the old Jackal and he linked arms in some alien hugging ritual.

"You are indebted no longer," the colonel responded. "This time when I escort you off this compound, it will be not as a fugitive but as a friend. I face no risk this time in allowing you to go."

Carly had given him her mossflower. It had gone willingly. She'd put her fingers in her hair, and it allowed itself to be plucked. When she'd hugged the colonel good-bye, the flower had nestled itself among the feathers on his lapel, like a boutonniere.

The mood in the landing craft was somber. Carly tried to focus on how happy Piper and Dash would be to learn that they had gotten more than enough

Stinger spores. She tried to look forward to telling the story of Gabriel's mad dash in the Simu Suit.

"So long, Infinity," Gabriel said as he hit the ignition. The *Cloud Cat* soared across the planet's surface, whipping by the Jackal compound and gaining altitude.

"Good-bye, Colonel," Carly whispered, pressing her hand to the window. She couldn't see him inside the compound, but if he was watching them leave on one of his monitors, she wanted him to see her waving.

The *Cloud Cat* zipped toward the *Cloud Leopard*, gaining altitude. Carly gazed down at the lonely gray surface. The landscape hadn't changed, but it looked so different to her now. The plain, stony surface masked so much—the darkness, the vibrancy, the thousands of living beings that teemed within the caves. They had been inside, and that changed everything.

Aboveground now, they had communication back. They radioed ahead to the *Cloud Leopard*, letting them know the landing craft was on approach.

"Mission: success. We're coming home," Gabriel reported.

"Great. I'm opening the landing bay doors." Dash's voice sounded strange and tight. Especially for a guy on the receiving end of such good news.

Gabriel felt a tiny clutch in his belly, but he pushed it aside.

Everything was fine.

Great, in fact.

His body still hummed with the adrenaline of dodging Stingers and fighting off Saws. It was probably just an overreaction.

Dash met them in the landing bay.

"Hey, man," Gabriel said, leaping out of the *Cloud Cat.* "We got them."

Chris held up the jar full of Stinger spores.

It should have been a moment of leaping and high fives. But Dash didn't even crack a smile. His serious expression brought the others up short.

Gabriel swallowed hard. The bad feeling in his stomach returned. "What is it?"

The first words out of Dash's mouth were "Piper's been kidnapped."

"What?" Carly gasped. "What are you talking about?"

"We got an SOS from the *Light Blade.*" Dash explained what had happened. He sighed heavily. "They tricked us. They're holding her hostage for the Gamma jump."

Gabriel's face clouded over. "No way. We'll go over there and get her back." He moved as if to get back in the *Cloud Cat.*

"We can't start fighting with the Omega crew," Dash said, grabbing Gabriel's arm.

Gabriel shook him off. "We already have a problem with them taking our stuff," he said angrily, thinking of the Weavers down in the tunnels.

"They started it, the minute they messed with Piper." Carly agreed with Gabriel. "We have no choice."

"Let's go upstairs," Dash said, keeping his voice level. He'd been doing nothing but thinking about Piper all day. The others were coming into the situation fresh and hot. Of course they would be fighting mad and ready to get Piper back by storm.

They didn't know what Dash knew. They didn't have the full perspective.

Dash glanced at Chris, who had been notably silent during the discussion thus far. His expression appeared almost totally blank.

On the flight deck, the argument continued.

"So we refuse to leave, until they give us Piper," Carly said. "And then we promise not to ditch them at Gamma Speed."

"They won't give her up. It'll turn into a standoff. We don't have that kind of time," Dash said. He alone knew his clock was running out. He glanced at Chris, who stared straight back at him, almost as if unseeing.

"They have to get back to Earth just as fast as we do," Carly argued. "And they can't get home without us. If we refuse to leave, they won't know we're bluffing."

"We can't afford to lose those days," Dash insisted.

The others glared at him, puzzled.

Carly was more than puzzled—she was furious. Was the mission really all Dash cared about? After all his big talk about teamwork? She couldn't believe what she was hearing.

Gabriel crossed his arms over his chest. No man gets left behind. They would always do what was necessary to save a friend in trouble. Hadn't they just proved that with Colonel Ramos in the Sawtooth den? And he wasn't even a member of their crew. But Dash was right about one thing—it would turn into a standoff.

"We'll have to do more than promise," Gabriel admitted. "I don't think they can believe we'd never ditch them in space. Because they would do it to us. They just proved that in the tunnels."

Chris finally spoke. "We haven't lost Piper. She's safe. It's not like we're leaving her behind."

"You would just take off and leave her with them?" Carly said. "For the whole next Gamma jump?" Her eyes blurred over, but she blinked the tears away. "That could be weeks."

Weeks that Dash didn't have. "I'm the mission commander," Dash said tightly. "And Chris is our guide. Our votes get extra weight."

"Not fair," Gabriel protested. "We need the fifth vote for a tiebreaker."

"Piper's vote," Carly whispered.

The crew stood in silence for a long moment. Carly stared at the screen that showed the *Light Blade* trailing them through orbit. For a moment on

Infinity, she had thought there was hope for Siena and Niko. Fighting off that Saw together had felt good. It was right to join forces. Eight against the universe would be much better than four. Being frenemies really was not working out. For anyone. Why couldn't the Omega crew see that?

The truth had to be spoken, so Carly said it. "Piper would vote to put the mission first," she told the others. "You know she would."

22

Niko, Ravi, and Siena returned to the *Light Blade* after the harrowing adventure. Their sacks full of Stingers had gone limp in the lack of moist air. They didn't get enough to make a thousand, unless the Stingers could be revived to produce more spores each.

"We'll have to humidify them somehow," Siena said.

"Put 'em in a little sauna?" Ravi suggested.

"Something like that," Niko agreed. "But who knows if they'll even make more spores in captivity."

"We should go back and release them into the caves," Siena argued. "If we bring them with us, they'll die."

"The ZRKs can build them an enclosure," Niko suggested. "We'll pump some steam in. They'll be okay."

The three tubed their way to the rec room. They tied the Stinger bags together there—better to work with them after the Gamma jump. As soon as the

Cloud Leopard was ready to go, the *Light Blade* had to follow within a short time or they'd lose the Gamma trail completely.

Anna was alone up on the *Light Blade* bridge when the *Cloud Leopard*'s message came through.

"We're jumping to Gamma Speed," Dash said. "Get ready to stick with us."

Anna smiled at him. "We're ready. See how nice it is when we can all get along?"

"Don't push it," Dash said. "We'll expect to see and talk to Piper first thing when we get to Tundra."

"We'll take good care of her," Anna promised. "She's our insurance policy, remember?"

Dash's jaw tightened. "Going to Gamma in five." He punched out and the screen went dark.

"Catch you on the flip side," Anna murmured to the empty screen.

The rest of the Omega crew made their way to the flight deck and strapped in for the Gamma jump. Down in the utility room, Colin released Piper's wrist restraints in order to strap her air chair securely to the ship.

Clearly, he didn't want her going anywhere.

"You could let me come up on the flight deck," she told him. "I'm not going to mess with anything."

"You're still a hostage," he answered. "You stay here."

The door slid shut behind him, leaving Piper

alone with the clicking and clunking sounds of the ship's machinery. She looked around the small space. It was barely more than a utility closet. Pipes and tubes lined the walls. The door was a thick sheet of metal.

Worst of all, there was only one reason she could think of for them to tie her to the ship. They were going to Gamma Speed.

Piper fought against the sudden sting behind her eyes. A Gamma jump would last weeks, or even months. Would she be a prisoner the entire time?

She hated this small room. Through the walls she could hear the engine noises . . . plus a hissing, rattling sound that didn't seem entirely normal. Then again, nothing was normal about this situation.

Once they were in Gamma Speed, she would convince them to untie her. There would be no reason not to. They couldn't very well keep her tied up for the next few weeks. At least she hoped not.

Piper's mind tripped toward her bigger worry. Would they release her on the next planet? Would she get to participate in any more retrievals, or was she going to be a captive for the remainder of the journey? On the one hand, she hoped Dash and the Alpha team would stage some sort of daring rescue, but on the other hand, she really did believe the mission should come first. The most important thing was getting the elements back to Earth in time.

She wanted to kick herself for her gullibility, though. Her role in the Voyagers mission may have come to a halt, all because she'd gone out of her way to help someone in need. Next time, she promised herself, she wouldn't be so foolish.

After the Gamma jump, everyone on the *Light Blade* relaxed. They could spend the next several weeks or more free from worry about getting lost in space or dodging strange creatures in unfamiliar terrain. Training for the challenges of Tundra would begin now.

"All right!" Ravi cheered. "Four planets down, two to go."

Siena also grinned. It felt good to shed the concerns that came with each planet adventure. She looked toward Niko, expecting to meet a smile in response.

Niko's face was pale. He stood perfectly still in the middle of the flight deck. He wasn't looking at the screen or at the crew. He stared straight ahead, as if unseeing.

"Niko?" Siena asked. A different kind of concern flashed through her. "Are you okay?"

He blinked several times. "Yeah, I . . . well, I . . ." He made a choking, gargling sound.

"Whoa, man," Ravi blurted out. "You don't look so good."

Niko stumbled forward, bracing himself against the back of a chair. Ravi and Siena leapt to his sides and caught him as he fell to the floor. Niko's eyes rolled back into his head, and his arms and shoulders twitched.

"Niko! Oh no," Siena cried. "What's happening?" She cradled Niko's head as Ravi tried to hold his flailing arms in place.

Anna leaned over them. "Is it a seizure?"

"Hurts," Niko groaned.

"Where?" Siena asked. "Where does it hurt?"

Niko pushed his chin toward his right shoulder. Ravi grasped the collar of Niko's uniform shirt and pulled it down over his arm.

Siena gasped. A red welt the size of a fingertip dug into the skin over Niko's shoulder socket. A Stinger spore had gotten through!

"Oh my God," Siena breathed. She exchanged a frightened glance with Ravi. This was bad. Really bad.

Tiny red lines radiated from the center of the wound as the poison leached further into Niko's system. "What do we do?" Ravi asked. "Dig out the spore? Try some kind of medicine?"

"I don't know," Anna snapped from above. "All they told us was that Stinger spore poison is fatal."

Siena felt the words like a fist around her heart. Ravi lowered his eyes.

Anna paced the room. "How could this happen?"

Colin, ever practical, said, "The mission was dangerous. We all knew that."

Niko passed out in Siena's arms. His body went limp.

"We can't just let him die!" Siena cried. "We have to try something."

"But Niko's our medic," Ravi said. "We'd kind of need him in order to help him."

"Well," Anna said, trying to keep the unsettledness out of her voice. She glanced at Colin. "Actually . . . we do have another medic on board."

Siena and Ravi turned to her. "What are you talking about?"

Anna cleared her throat. "We have a guest below-decks." She punched a button, and the screen showed Piper strapped in place in the utility closet. "A little insurance policy so the *Cloud Leopard* crew doesn't try anything tricky."

Siena was horrified. "You kidnapped Piper?"

The flight deck fell into silence as the crew processed this information.

Ravi shrugged. "Makes sense. They definitely won't ditch us now."

Siena glanced from the incriminating image on the screen to Niko's limp body sprawled across her lap.

On the screen, Piper's eyes searched the room

as if looking for an escape option. Siena grew angry looking at Piper's distressed face. "That's horrible. I can't believe it. Where is she?" It was hard to determine the room from the close-up image.

Anna and Siena stared at each other for a long moment. Not exactly a battle of wills, since Anna was in charge, but the flight deck fell silent as the girls faced off.

Siena remained crouched beside the collapsed Niko, holding him in her arms. Anna stood over her.

"Where is she?" Siena shouted. "I'll go get her!"

"The Stinger serum is fatal," Ravi said. "There's really no point."

"We have to try," Siena said. If Piper could give them any chance of saving Niko's life, then maybe, *maybe* Siena could live with what Anna and Colin had done. If some good could come of it . . .

"Please." The word was already on Siena's lips as Anna turned away, rushing from the flight deck.

Anna raced through the ship's corridors toward the utility closet. *This is stupid,* she thought. *It's only prolonging the inevitable.* And yet she found herself running as fast as she could.

It hurt to hope for the impossible. But everything about the Omega crew's mission was already on the edge of impossible.

She threw open the utility closet door. The blond girl strapped motionlessly into her seat looked startled as the mission commander burst into her small would-be prison cell.

"Piper," Anna said breathlessly. "We need your help."

Find the Source. Save the World.

Follow the Voyagers to the next planet!

SIGN ON. JOIN THE CREW. SAVE THE WORLD!

VOYAGERS

5

ESCAPE THE VORTEX

JEANNE DuPRAU

New York Times bestselling author of *The City of Ember*

Carly and Dash sat still for a moment, gazing out at the Tundra landscape. Wind whistled around them and blew spirals of snow into the air. Carly spoke into her transmitter, and Dash heard her voice as if she were speaking right next to his ear. "First on the agenda," she said. "The cave."

"Right," said Dash. He checked his MTB and read out the coordinates that Chris had provided.

Carly pressed a button, and the motor roared. The Streak leaned and turned. Dash could see nothing but white, white, and more white as they sped along, until suddenly a strip of black rock would rear up and be gone, or they'd pass a snowdrift shaped by the wind into peaks with blue shadows. Ridges of jagged ice, cliffs that seemed to rise out of nowhere—it was a rugged landscape, where fast travel was perilous.

And yet Carly kept the racer moving at incredible speed. "I love this!" she cried. She ran the Streak up a slope and over the top, and for a few seconds, they were airborne. "Wheee!"

When they'd been speeding along for five or six minutes, Dash noticed that they were picking up a heat signal. "Slow down for a minute," he said. "Something's out there."

Carly braked. "What is it?"

"I don't know. Look at this reading." He held out his wrist.

"Maybe an ice crawler?"

"I don't think so. This thing is moving faster than any animal would."

Carly changed course, and they headed toward the signal. It wasn't long before they saw a dark dot speeding across the landscape. It could be only one thing.

"The *Light Blade* team," Dash said. "They got here before us."

Carly's voice sounded grim in Dash's ear. "All right," she said, "they're here, but they haven't found the cave. They're in the wrong place. We'll get there before them."

She stepped on the accelerator. The engine

roared and screamed as Carly swung around a sharp curve.

Dash's heart was racing—full of adrenaline. *This is awesome,* he thought, but the next moment, when he glanced down at the map, a shock ran through him. "Carly, look out! Straight ahead—a crevasse! Slow down!"

Carly veered sharp right. The brakes squealed, and the racer stopped in a cloud of snow. They turned to look at each other, wide-eyed. Carly moved the Streak forward an inch at a time, until they were right at the edge of the great crack in the ice—sheer walls of deep blue plunged to an invisible bottom.

They were silent for a moment.

"We can do it easily," Carly said.

"You're sure?"

"Sure. I've jumped wider ones a hundred times on the simulator. We just have to get up speed. Come on."

She turned the Streak and drove it back the way they'd come for half a mile, then turned again in the direction of the crevasse. Dash watched the speedometer—sixty miles per hour, sixty-five, seventy—and then looked through the windshield to see the lip of the yawning crack straight ahead, and suddenly, there was air beneath them, deep blue fathoms of it. But before he knew it, the white ground was below them again, the landing so smooth and soft he hardly felt it.

Carly grinned and kept going. Dash gave her a quick, happy punch in the arm.

For a while, they sped across the snow easily, like expert skiers, riding the curves, catching air on the high dunes, never slackening their speed. Dash sat back; his tension drained away.

They crested a hill, and Dash looked out toward the horizon and saw pale, cloudlike columns rising against the sky, dipping and twirling and bending like mile-high dancers. They moved together, in an unruly crowd, maybe fifty of them, maybe more, sweeping across the snowy land toward a region of low hills.

"Uh-oh," said Carly. "Look." She pointed to the west, where a line of darkness showed above the mountains.

"A storm," said Dash. "Do you think we're headed for it?"

"I think it's headed for us," Carly answered, and immediately, Dash could see that it was. The dark line was rising, covering more and more of the sky.

"The wind's picking up," Carly said. "I can feel it trying to blow us sideways." She tightened her grip on the steering wheel.

Snow struck against the windshield, hard, like

little pebbles, and the clouds came lower, and then they were inside the blizzard. Wind drove the snow at them in a blinding spiral.

"I can't see anything!" Carly wrestled with the steering wheel, trying to steady the Streak against the wind howling around them. "We have to slow down."

Dash pressed against the glass, squinting, trying to see through the swirling white. "Looks like a gap in the cliff up ahead," he said, pointing. "Can we get there?"

"I don't know!" Carly's voice had an edge of fear. "This wind! It's so strong!"

The noise was thunderous. A powerful gust struck them from the side, and Dash felt the Streak tipping him toward the ground. "We're going over!" he shouted.

Carly fought hard, but when the wind caught their underside, it pushed full force, and the snowmobile leaned and fell, leaving them sitting sideways, strapped into their seats, one above the other. The driver's side door was now the roof door.

Carly clicked its lock and pushed upward with all her might. The door sprang open, letting in showers of snow. "Climbing out!" Carly radioed. She undid her seat belt and gripped the edge of the door and hoisted herself through, feeling a moment of gratitude for all those pull-ups STEAM had made her do. Lying across the Streak's side, she stretched an arm down toward Dash. He grabbed her hand, she pulled, and he made his way up and out.

What struck him first was not the wind, not the driving snow, but the cold. It seemed to come right through his protective suit and find its way into his bones. He was stunned by it.

They both were.

But they had to move. They dropped down to ground level and stood beside the Streak, which lay with its runners facing them. "Grab the top runner," Dash said. Carly did, and he did too, and they both pulled on it with all their strength. But the Streak, though it ran across snow as lightly as a water spider, was built of heavy stuff, and they couldn't budge it. They walked around it and tried hoisting it up from the other side. "Look," said Carly, "this whole part is already frozen into the snow."

If they'd had a long board and a rock, they might have made a lever to lift the Streak, but Tundra was treeless. If they'd had a way to boil water, they might have freed the Streak by melting the ice that held it. But though they had water with them, they had no stove to heat it on. "We could make a fire," said Dash, but without hope. What fire would survive in this wind?

They heard some scraping sounds, and in the open hatch of the Streak, a trapezoidal head appeared.

"TULIP!" cried Carly. "We forgot her!"

They lifted up TULIP's heavy little body and set her down on the snow. Her belly glowed orange.

"Good call, Carly!" shouted Dash.

Carly smiled. "The cold never bothered me anyway."

TULIP was already at work. Heat beamed out from her middle at the ice locking the Streak to the ground, and in a few minutes, the ice was water. Dash and Carly slid their fat-gloved hands underneath, found the ridge at the top of the window, and pulled with all their might. When the ship came free, they backed up to it and pushed with the force of their whole bodies. The Streak groaned, creaked, and at last sat upright on its runners.

Carly cheered. "Done!" she cried out. "Let's go!"

But Dash stood still. A wave of weakness swept over him. His body felt heavy as stone. He couldn't show Carly he was breaking down, so he leaned against a snowbank and pretended to be tinkering with his wrist tech settings. "Hold on a second," he said. "I need to make an adjustment here." His heart was pounding at his ribs—thud, thud, thud—way too fast.

"What adjustment? What's wrong?"

"Just have to get these coordinates . . ." *Breathe,* he told himself.

"Do it while we ride!" yelled Carly. "We have to hurry!"

But it was several seconds before Dash could make his legs move. By the time he got into the Streak and fastened his straps, Carly was vibrating with impatience. "I don't understand what took so long," she said.

Dash spoke as strongly as he could, which was hard, knowing he was lying. "I had to get the settings right. It's tough to do it when we're going a thousand miles an hour."

For a second, they scowled at each other.

But there was no time for that. The next second, they were off again, moving slowly at first through the diminishing storm, and then fast as the storm passed over them and they came into the clear.

Carly resumed top speed. They followed the route through the valley, climbed toward the mountain pass, and after some wrong turns and mistaken stops, they came to the dark mouth of a cave at the top of a long, boulder-strewn slope. It would have been a moment to celebrate except for one thing: the snowmobile from the *Light Blade* was already there.

Gabriel stood at the console of the *Cloud Leopard*'s navigation deck, watching a dot on a screen that showed the *Cloud Cat*'s progress toward Tundra. The dot moved down and down. A yellow starburst flared. That was the landing. The *Cloud Cat* was dropping off Dash and Carly. A few minutes later, another yellow burst signaled that the *Cloud Cat* was on its way back. Good. Time to go and have a talk with Chris.

He hopped into the nearest portal and sped through the maze. In seconds, he was at the other end of the ship, tumbling out onto the floor of the engine room. He waited, and soon he heard the outer door of the docking bay opening, the transport ship powering down and rolling in, and the outer door closing. For a moment, there was quiet, and then the inner door slid upward and in came the *Cloud Cat*. Chris climbed down from the cockpit.

Gabriel bounded toward him. "Did everything go okay?"

"Yeah," said Chris. "No problems."

"Pretty cold down there?"

"You can't imagine. All okay here?"

"Fine. It's only been about half an hour since you left." Gabriel grinned. "Not a lot can go wrong in half an hour."

"Well, actually it can," said Chris. "But I'm glad it didn't."

They walked together out of the bay and up the central corridor. "I expect they'll be able to get the element in five hours or so," Chris said. "If all goes well. There's the weather to contend with, of course, and there could be some trouble dealing with the ice crawlers. But this mission ought to be a fairly quick one."

Gabriel checked the time on his MTB. "So it's eight thirty right now. That means they should be calling in at about one thirty with the signal for one of us to pick them up."

"That's right," said Chris. "And in the meantime, will you be okay on your own? A few hours of free time won't be unwelcome, I'm sure."

"I think I can suffer through them," Gabriel said.

"See you later, then. I have to go and check on—" Chris paused awkwardly. "Various matters."

"Before you go," said Gabriel, putting a hand on Chris's arm. "I have an idea. Can we talk for a second?"

"Sure. In here?" Chris led Gabriel into the rec room, and they sat down at one of the small tables. Someone had left a bagel there. "Want this?" Gabe asked, and when Chris shook his head, he picked it up and took a bite.

"So what's the idea?" Chris asked.

"We have to get Piper back," said Gabriel, chewing.

"Correct," said Chris. "Dash and I have been negotiating about it with Anna, but we haven't gotten anywhere so far."

"We have to get it done," said Gabe, "whether Anna agrees or not."

"You're right, of course. But how do we do that?"

"We go and get her," Gabriel said with a mouthful of bagel. "We take the *Cloud Cat*. We fly it right up to the *Light Blade*, and we board the ship, kind of like pirates, only *good* pirates. We find Piper, and we rescue her. Now."

"Ah," said Chris. He gave Gabriel a serious look. "But I don't see how that would work."

Gabriel put the bagel down. "Why not?"

"For one thing, how would we get the *Cloud Cat* into the *Light Blade*? I doubt that the team is just going to open up the dock doors for us."

"There must be a way."

"There will be a way," said Chris, "but I'm pretty sure that won't be it." He pushed back his chair and stood up.

"What *will* it be, then?"

"I don't know yet," said Chris. "But acting like pirates isn't it. We need a diplomatic approach." He turned and started for the door. "See you in a few hours."

Okay, thought Gabriel. His conscience was clear. He'd run his idea (most of it) by Chris, but Chris didn't like it. Chris was wrong on this one. They had a chance to rescue Piper right now, and they couldn't let this chance go by. Gabriel would just have to do it himself.